FAR APART

J LAUREL NELSON

Far Apart by J Laurel Nelson

www.jlaurelnelson.com

Cover by Damonza.com
Map by Madeline Nelson

978-1-7320178-0-1 Trade Paperback
978-1-7320178-1-8 Hardcover
978-1-7320178-2-5 Kindle e-book

For my daughters.

CHAPTER ONE

THE TRICK

SOMETHING ABOUT THE way Myree stood frozen in place made Kraster doubt his decision. He could tell she didn't want him to go, but she'd said she understood. It was too late now anyway. They'd used the rope Wilton brought to tie Kraster onto Wilton's back. Kraster's shoulders were lined up so that he could help push down on Wilton's arms supporting the long glide down off the mesa.

"I'll try to find a way back up, okay Myree? I promise."

"I'll try to find a way to climb down too."

Kraster smiled at the thought of his eight-year-old sister trying to find a climbing route down the cliffs, but he knew why she said it. He loved her too.

"Goodbye."

"See you later."

Wilton was on all fours now and ready to go. His ears were already folded back. He took a few steps closer to the cliff and let the patagiums between his arms and legs relax and loosen. Kraster noticed Wilton's reddish fur flattening and felt a shiver course through his own body.

"You ready, Kraster?"

"I'm ready." He spoke instinctively, without meaning it.

They both glanced a farewell at Myree, Wilton nodding and Kraster smiling, then Wilton ran the last five meters and jumped off the cliff. He stretched out his arms and legs turning the normally loose skin between them into tight sails. They had practiced the jump on a smaller ridge several times earlier in the day, so the initial drop was not unexpected, but the distance to the forests below was shocking. They glided out away from the cliff at terrific speed.

"The wind hurts my eyes. Let's take turns - what do you think?" Wilton shouted to be heard as he and Kraster glided down toward the blanket of green that surrounded the mesa. Since no one had ever managed to climb back up to the mesa, no one had warned them it would be so hard to keep their eyes open on the way down.

"Okay. Who's first?"

"I'm closing my eyes now. As soon as I give them a chance to recover I'll open them and tell you. Then you close your eyes and tell me when you reopen them. Okay?"

"Okay." Kraster could hardly hear Wilton, but he thought he understood. If he ever made it back up to the mesa, he would tell everyone about this so they'd be ready. It occurred to him that every jumper must have thought the same thing.

"Your turn!", shouted Wilton.

Kraster closed his eyes and waited for the burning to subside. He wanted to rub them but he was determined to keep steady downward pressure on Wilton's arms. The rope had seemed tight on the rim but now he wished it was a little tighter. Maybe it had something to do with the way larrens stretched out to glide. If he fell off, he was dead. He added that to the list of things he would tell everyone if he ever made it back up to the mesa.

"Your turn. I'm opening my eyes."

Kraster looked out through squinted eyes and still had to blink constantly. The forest was noticeably closer than it had been just thirty seconds ago. They were close enough to the ground that he could see the individual trees clearly but he couldn't see any fields or meadows where they could land. They continued to take turns and Kraster thought it was like going down steps. Every time he opened his eyes they had taken another step down. The base around the mesa had looked rugged from the rim, but it looked more rugged the further they dropped. They were running out of time and needed a place to land.

Larrens could glide for a relatively short window of their youth. When they were very young, they weren't strong enough, and when they grew older, they became too heavy. There was a period where they were strong enough and light enough to glide to the forest below; as long as they had a little help from a human. Not just anyone. The human had to be strong enough that they could help push down on the larren's arms for the long glide down, but light enough that they didn't just make it worse.

"I think I see an opening. Go to the left a little." Kraster's voice felt powerless against the wind, but Wilton must have heard him.

"I see it. We better try it; I can't last much longer."

"Me neither."

It wasn't much of an opening, but it would have to work. Kraster was trying to gauge their approach. "Can you slow down?"

“I’m trying. I need more help.”

Kraster wasn’t sure if he was pushing harder than he had been before. His arms shook with exhaustion, but he pushed down over and over.

“I’m going to miss it.” shouted Wilton.

“What?” But Wilton didn’t respond. There was nothing to say as they glided over the small meadow going much faster than either of them would have liked. Until that moment, Kraster hadn’t seriously considered the possibility that they might crash. In the space of a few seconds it had become almost certain, and for the first time in his life he expected to die. It was a surprising mix of fear and calm. The fear filled his whole body, but there was nothing he could do and he remained frozen on Wilton’s back staring ahead at the terrifying forest. They dropped lower until they hit the branches of a tall narrow tree. The impact was shocking. They snapped off the top quarter of the trunk, slashed through the high branches of several other trees, and finally slammed into a tree trunk that didn’t break. The rope kept Kraster trapped against Wilton’s back, but it probably saved his life. They fell through the branches, breaking some and bouncing off others, until they hit the ground on their side.

“Are you okay?” Kraster needed to untie the rope that was digging into his skin, but only his left arm was free and sharp pain shot up through his shoulder when he tried to move it. “Wilton! Are you okay?” There was no answer and Kraster slipped out of consciousness.

CHAPTER TWO

MYREE'S GUILT

Myree stood staring at the last spot she had seen Kraster and Wilton. She had watched them get smaller and smaller until they were a tiny moving dot against the green and brown of the base. Her body shook as another wave of sadness rolled through her mind but she fought to hold back the tears. Once she started crying there was no way she would be able to see them and there was no one in the world she loved more than her brother. Even as an eight-year-old, she knew that the only way she would ever see Kraster again was to glide down herself with a young larren.

That was assuming Kraster and Wilton survived the landing. Not everyone did. The jumpers would always make a fire after they landed to let those on the mesa know they made it. About one time in twenty, there was no fire. There was no question the young larrens could glide; they practiced all the time on the wind-swept mesa. But that was for a few hundred meters, not several kilometers. There was no trial run for the big jump.

They were out of sight for good and she felt the tears

grow in her eyes as her reason for fighting them disappeared. Somewhere a couple thousand meters below her, Wilton and Kraster would be looking for a place to land. Their arms were probably exhausted. She wondered whether they were excited or terrified right now. Within a few minutes, they would either be safe on the ground, injured, or dead. If she were older, she would go find a larren right now and make the jump, but the larrens had a rule that they would never ask someone younger than sixteen to make the jump with them. Kraster was only ten and a half but this had been a special case. Wilton said it had taken three weeks of secret negotiation, but that ultimately both the larren and human councils had approved the jump. None of the younger larrens could be trusted with the message and Wilton was getting old enough that he needed to compensate for his weight by partnering with a younger human.

Myree looked for a comfortable place to sit. It could be several hours before they got their fire built so she settled down to wait. Going home didn't sound very appealing anyway. Her parents were going to be devastated, even if this was an important mission. With a little luck, the Council would have already told them by the time she got home.

Seven hours later, a search party found her sitting at the cliffs in the dark and her story tore across the mesa like a winter windstorm. They'd brought her home where she spent the next two hours answering questions. It was past midnight, but every few minutes someone else would show up at their door wanting to talk to her and her parents. She didn't understand everything people were saying but it was clear that Kraster didn't have permission to make the jump. Or more accurately, Wilton didn't have permission. No one was blaming Kraster;

everyone was mad at Wilton, and it felt like she was being grouped with Wilton.

When she wasn't being interviewed, the visitors talked amongst themselves with greater agitation as the night progressed. Many of them wanted to build a wall around town to keep larrens from stealing any more children.

Her parents were angry and heartbroken, just like she'd known they would be. And it felt like they were a little mad at her too. It reminded her of the time she had fallen backwards in her chair a year ago and broken three of their plates. Her parents said they knew she didn't try to break the plates on purpose, but her Mom in particular was still annoyed. And now, they knew she didn't want Kraster to make the jump, but she was still involved and they seemed angry.

She kept answering the same questions over and over. The worst question had only come up once, but the sting of it lingered. "Why didn't you try to stop them?" Her parents had jumped to her defense - she was only eight - how could she have known? But now she wondered. Why hadn't she tried to stop them?

She didn't know what time it was, but her dad had finally had enough and herded everyone out of their home, telling them to come back tomorrow. He carried her to her room and it was the first hug that felt real since they found her at the cliffs.

"I'm sorry Daddy. I didn't know."

"Oh Myree. Sweetheart. It's not your fault. It's really not your fault. You didn't do anything wrong. Do you understand?"

"Yes Daddy."

"We've kept you up so late! Try to sleep now. We can talk about this more tomorrow. Are you tired?"

"Mmhmm."

He tucked her in and gave her the two kisses on each cheek that always finished the day.

"Mom will come in to say goodnight in just a minute. I love you Myree. Sleep well."

"Love you too."

Myree lay staring at the ceiling and trying desperately to stay awake until her Mom got there. Despite the sorrow of losing Kraster, she had been excited to stay up so late. But her eyes kept closing and she kept willing them open. Her mom slipped quietly into the room and sat beside her on the bed.

"You're still awake? You must be so tired. Myree darling, you know this isn't your fault don't you?"

"I know. I don't know why I didn't stop them." Saying the words out loud was more than her heart could bear and the guilt she felt overflowed in tears.

Her mom pulled back the blanket and wrapped Myree in her arms as she climbed in beside her. She kissed her forehead over and over.

"It wasn't your job to stop them. I'm sorry you've been dragged into this whole mess. Wilton is the only one to blame. Not Kraster and not you. It wasn't your fault."

They held each other until they both stopped crying and fell asleep.

CHAPTER THREE

THE SMALLEST INCREMENT

KRASTER OPENED HIS eyes and watched the tree branches swaying slowly to a warm August breeze he couldn't feel. Someone had moved him. He was lying on his back with his head propped up slightly. Both of his arms and his left leg were bound with splints, and there was a strange taste on the tip of his tongue that filled his mouth and tingled down his throat when he swallowed. He tried to roll over and gasped in pain.

"It's okay. Try to stay still. You're hurt pretty bad, but you'll be okay." The woman who spoke had been sitting nearby and now stood and walked over. "I tried to patch you up as best I could, but it's a little tough to figure out what needs patching when the patient can't talk. Where does it hurt the most?"

"Everywhere hurts."

"Can you move your fingers for me?" Kraster obeyed, suddenly scared and curious to know if he could. "Good. How about your right foot? Don't try to move your left leg if you can help it. That was the worst break. Well that's good to see. I assume your neck is sore, but does it feel like it's seriously injured?"

"No, it feels fine. I mean, it doesn't feel seriously injured."

"Good. I really want you to lay still but I'm going to pour some water in your mouth when you're ready. Ready?"

Kraster nodded and swallowed a mouthful at a time. The woman helping him looked like she might be a few years older than his mother. She had brown eyes that were dark at the edges and lighter toward the middle, with little hints of green mixed in. She had short hair that he guessed she cut herself. There was a roughness about her. Not roughness like meanness, more like toughness.

"That's probably enough for now. Your body needs rest. Close your eyes and try to sleep if you can."

"Who are you?"

"My name's Cindl. What's yours?"

"Kraster." Talking hurt his chest. "How's Wilton?"

"Wilton's the larren you came down with?"

"Yeah."

"Well, his injuries are much worse than yours. It doesn't look good." She paused trying to decide whether to keep going or let Kraster sleep. "How old are you?"

"I'm ten and a half. I know that's too young, but Wilton had a secret message he was supposed to deliver and he had special permission to ask me."

"Okay. Now this time I'm serious - close your eyes and sleep." Cindl could feel her anger rising and wanted to end the conversation in case Kraster thought it was directed at him. She had made the jump herself about fifteen years ago when she was seventeen. And as far as she could remember, this larren called Wilton looked like he was too big to have been approved for the jump. It was clear that a desperate and selfish larren had fooled a kid into leaving his family on the mesa. She could still remember liking larrens when she was a kid, but everything changed after the jump. The larrens on the base were colder and more distant. They were usually civil when you met them, but she rarely did. Even her childhood friend Lina left after they made the jump together. The larrens lived in their own town and she'd never talked to her again. Admittedly, her decision to live so far from everyone else didn't help anything. But there was no escaping the obvious; after the jump, the larrens didn't need humans.

Once Kraster had fallen asleep, she walked back over to Wilton. He had remained unconscious since she found them four hours earlier. That he was alive at all was incredible. Even if she could move him, she'd be scared to try. There was a large broken tree branch sticking out of his side and his body was covered in deep cuts. As angry as she was, it was obvious the larren had taken almost all the damage from the impact, and she wondered if he may have taken that impact on purpose to protect Kraster.

She stuffed another wad of laddenweed into his cheek to dull the pain and his eyes flickered open. His gaze darted around but he seemed to know instinctively not to move; or maybe he couldn't.

"Is Kraster dead?" He said it almost as a fact; as if he was trying to prepare his mind for a bad answer.

"No, Kraster's hurt, but I think he'll survive." At least he had the decency to ask about Kraster first. Her anger receded by the smallest of increments. "He told me he's ten years old."

Wilton closed his eyes and they never opened again. "Yes, I know. I'm so sorry. I never should have asked him."

"You mean you never should have tricked him?"

"Yes."

"Would you like some water?" But this time there was no answer.

CHAPTER FOUR
BETTER THIS WAY

OVER THE NEXT four weeks, Cindl adopted Kraster. Not formally, but she decided she would be the person to protect him until he turned sixteen. She liked him. He was respectful, kind, and had a confidence that was too deep-rooted to be an act. And he was smart for a ten-year-old. Still, Wilton's death was hard on him. He would talk about almost anything, but if Cindl brought up Wilton, he would retreat. She didn't know if it was just the trauma of the death, the horrific crash, or if he suspected Wilton had lied to him. If Wilton hadn't died so recently she would tell him, but it seemed rude somehow; disrespectful.

Kraster was feeling much better. The broken bones in his arms and left leg were healing well. He had also broken at least two ribs and she suspected the long scar on his neck would be permanent. Cindl's father had been a doctor on the mesa and she had helped him right up until the day before her own jump. She knew the bones would still be vulnerable to a re-break, but they were both getting restless sitting around their campsite. She made Kraster promise to go slow - no jumping or climbing

- then they packed up and started a slow trek upland toward the villages along the base of the cliffs.

It was difficult terrain. The base rose in fits and starts upwards from the desert until it ended abruptly at the cliffs. There were thousands of small streams that either trickled down the cliffs or emerged as springs near the bottom, and they had carved up the base over the millennia. Forests coated the landscape and got thicker as they climbed higher. Kraster had his own stream of questions and Cindl enjoyed seeing the base and cliffs again through fresh eyes. They were passing through a transition where some of the higher elevation trees started to appear in the forest and Kraster was jubilant as his mind processed an entirely new idea. The mesa was too flat for anything similar.

Kraster led the way, mostly because he liked it, but it also made talking easier. He would throw a quick question over his shoulder and then listen to Cindl's longer explanation.

"So, how close to the desert did you live?"

"That's a little complicated. Some of the rivers that flow out into the desert carve beautiful canyons before they fan out and disappear into the sand. I lived in one of those canyons along the last remnants of the Del river. The riverbed was dry most of the time. It only had water on the surface after a big rain on the mesa, but there was always water if you dug down a meter or two. Oh, and the canyon! I remember the first time I found it. I had headed out into the desert - just to explore a little. Anyway, I had no idea the canyon was out there and when I came to the edge and looked down, I knew I had found my new home. All around me were desert shrubs and rocks, but below me was a river of green trees and lighter green meadows. Breathtaking. I think that's what I loved about it. It was the contrast. It was this beautiful forest hidden at the edge of a harsh desert. My favorite walk was partly through trees and grass and partly in the desert. I would start out heading away from the riverbed, through my orchard, climb up the west side of the canyon, and then follow the rim out away from the mesa. On my left I would be looking down into a garden of life and on my right and straight ahead to the horizon was the desert. Near my house, the canyon is - how do I describe it - it's obvious. There's the riverbed, and the trees, and then the canyon walls. Very neat. But if you follow the river down into the desert, the canyon turns into a disorganized jumble. The trees disappear and you just have shrubs and grasses weaving through the maze of rocks. I would always try to drop back down somewhere new, and then I'd turn back up the riverbed. There was one curve in the canyon when you saw the first stand of trees, and then the trees would just keep growing thicker and larger all the time."

"I can't decide if I'd like the desert. It doesn't sound very nice."

"I'll have to take you out sometime so you can decide."

"Does anyone live out there?"

"I don't think anyone can live all the way out in the desert. You need some water. But Old Man Dorver was downstream from me almost an hour's walk. It's way out there; past the jumble of rocks where the riverbed really fans out. He says he likes it. He can still get to water with a ten meter well and manages to grow enough food. I almost never saw him."

"You didn't visit him?"

"When someone sets up that far out, it's because they don't want visitors. He's a very kind old man as far as I can tell, but he wants to be alone. I never asked him why."

"Is that why you moved so far out on the fringe?"

Cindl paused to think. There was something in the honesty of the question that pleaded for an honest answer. "Yes, I think that's basically true. I do love the beauty of it too, but I wanted to be alone. And hold on! Stop. I'm not going to tell you why I wanted to be alone. Adults are allowed to keep some secrets."

"Kids can have secrets too."

"Yes, you're right. Sometimes we keep them for very different reasons though. Should we change the subject?" It wasn't really a question.

"I guess." They walked in silence for several minutes while Kraster thought of a new topic. "So where are we going to live once we get to Lin?"

"Well, I'm not planning to live in Lin itself. We'll look for a meadow near Lin that we can turn into a farm."

"Are there too many people in Lin?"

"We agreed to change the subject, remember?" Kraster smiled and let her continue. "I doubt Lin has grown much since I was there last, so we shouldn't have too much trouble finding a good spot. I'm imagining something that's anywhere from a one to six hour walk from Lin."

"Can we try to find one close to the cliffs? I promised Myree I'd try to find a way back up to the mesa."

"We can look. The better meadows are usually a little farther from the cliffs. But if we can find one we like that's close, I'm all for it."

"Are you going to miss the fringe?"

"I think I will. I miss it right now. Do you miss the mesa?"

Kraster wasn't ready for the question and his voice had a

more serious tone when he answered. “I don’t miss the mesa, but I miss my family.”

Cindl waited for more but he was done. That was something she was still getting used to about Kraster. Often, if he could capture the core thought with one sentence, he didn’t have the impulse to elaborate with a second or third. It was a rare quality, and it usually surprised her.

“I know what you mean. I miss my sister. My parents and I weren’t on very good terms when I jumped and I wish I could make that right, but my sister and I were so close. She was three years younger than me and I was sure she would come down when she turned sixteen. I spent her sixteenth birthday sitting outside watching for her. But she never came. I can imagine a thousand good reasons why she didn’t come down, but it still hurt me that she didn’t; that she chose the mesa instead of me.”

“Did she ever send a message down with another pair?”

“No. It’s funny, but that doesn’t bother me as much. Before I made the jump I assumed my family would send me messages, but once I got down here… I guess it feels pointless. If they sent me some big news or just a greeting, there’s no way for me to respond. It’s the worst thing about those cliffs.”

“I know. My family probably thinks I’m dead and there’s no way to tell them I’m not.”

“Kraster, I’m so sorry I forgot to build the signal fire. I still can’t believe I forgot.”

“You were saving my life. I’m not mad at you. I just wish there was a way to fix it. But maybe it’s better this way. If Myree thinks I’m dead, she won’t leave Mom and Dad and follow me down.”

“You don’t want her to come?”

"I mean, yes, I'd like her to come, but I don't think she should. It's too dangerous."

They set up camp for the night on a low ridge with great views of both the cliffs and the desert behind them. After all these years, Cindl still loved watching the fading sunlight and shadows move up the cliffs until only the top was illuminated. Then, as the last rays spilled over the top of the cliffs and the darkness really settled on the base, the stars would begin their slow glorious dance across the sky.

CHAPTER FIVE

THE NEW GAME

KRASTER HAD JUMPED with Wilton a year ago and the mesa was completely changed. Myree's parents hadn't let her out of their sight for the first six months. Now the first wall was finished and she was allowed to walk to and from school on her own again. It was an impressive wall, she had to admit, but she hated it. She was trapped, with no way to fulfill her promise to Kraster. She hadn't even seen a larren since Wilton and she wondered when she would again. There had never been very many larrens in town, but in the past there were always a few running errands or selling something in the center circle. And there were always a lot of larrens down along the river.

The river didn't have a name, probably because it was the only one on the mesa. It divided the mesa roughly in half before cutting a deep slice in the southeastern edge. It rained almost every evening as the hot air from the desert was forced upward by the base and cliffs. The humans had lived on the southwestern half of the river as long as anyone could remember and the larrens lived on the other. The river was the one place they truly shared and she loved her memories of playing along the river with other human kids and young larrens.

That life was over. She was not allowed to go outside the wall; even with her parents. There had been a remembrance assembly for Kraster, and everyone talked about him in the past tense. But Myree wasn't sure. Maybe they were just hurt and couldn't light a signal fire, or they landed behind a ridge and their fire couldn't be seen from the mesa. She had asked about these possibilities early on, but it was obvious that they terrified her parents. For months she couldn't understand why they would want to think Kraster was dead. Then it hit her; they only wanted Myree to think he was dead. They wanted her to forget her promise. So that was the new game - she started pretending he was dead and that she would never leave.

CHAPTER SIX

MORE THAN ANYTHING

FOUR YEARS AND eleven months passed and Kraster grew up. He was fifteen now and tall for his age. His first few years had been rough. No other pairs glided down after him, and although no one knew exactly why, it was assumed that Kraster's gullibility was the root cause. It was the type of stigma that could have stuck with him for the rest of his life, but Kraster out-grew it. He wasn't popular in a social sense, but almost everyone admired him. A big part of that was his reputation as a climber. Cindl had settled on a long narrow meadow close to the cliffs for their farmstead and Kraster had been climbing almost every afternoon since they got there. There were only a handful of climbers who were still better than him, and every few weeks a new story would circulate through town about some amazing stunt he'd done on the cliffs. And even though everyone still agreed he probably should have known better than to glide down with Wilton, there was no escaping the fact that Wilton had singled him out. Of all the ten year olds, Wilton thought Kraster would give him the best chance of making the jump.

It was a beautiful July afternoon and Kraster motioned at a few good spots to sit, letting Cindl pick first. They were high above the forest on Kraster's favorite climbing route. There were other routes that went much higher, but as far as he knew, no one else had found this one. It led to a perfect little outcropping where you could sit and rest. In almost five years of climbing, this was the best place he'd found.

Cindl was impressed. "I love it! Wow, the view is…, well, it's just beautiful. I sometimes forget how beautiful it is from the cliffs. No one else knows about this spot?"

"I don't think so. I've never seen anyone else up here and, you probably weren't watching, but there aren't any climber marks. Except that K behind you, but that's mine. Every other route I've climbed has climber marks all over the place."

"If anyone could find a completely new route, it would be you. Well done!"

"Thank you." Kraster gave a small bow and failed to suppress his grin.

"When did you find this?"

"It was shortly after the first time we went out to check on your house in the canyon. So I guess I was probably twelve."

"You've kept this a secret that long? I can't imagine doing that. I would've told all my friends and they would have told all their friends… You get the idea."

"You should climb more often. You're pretty good for-"

"Were you really going to say 'an old woman'?"

"Sorry, you know what I meant. You really are pretty good at this."

"When I first got down here I used to climb all the time. I wasn't as famous as you, but I made enough crazy jumps that I'm amazed I'm still around."

"When did you stop?"

"I don't remember exactly. I climbed for several years, then it trailed off, and then one day I just never came back. I suppose I gave up and decided to focus on my new life."

"You think I should give up?"

"Oh, that's up to you. I didn't mean to suggest you should."

"I'd like to go around the mesa."

"Someone warned me you'd been talking about it."

"I've tried every route between The Knife and Echo Canyon, and I can't find a way up. I either have to give up or go try the cliffs beyond the boundaries. The cliffs around here are too steep and smooth. We all know it. For the last two years, all my climbing has just felt like practice for when I'm ready to find a better spot."

"No one ever comes back."

"Is that really true? I mean, I don't get it. How can we not know what happens to the people that leave? The forest looked the same in all directions from the mesa. If there was some creature out there that attacked the wanderers, why don't they ever come here? That can't be it."

"But think about it. Did you ever see the forest on the northeast side of the mesa? The larrens had their towns along that half of the rim and they didn't let humans go very far into their territory. I have no idea what's on the other side of the mesa; none of us do."

"That's true, but we could definitely see part of the base past The Knife and Echo Canyon. It all looked the same. Have you ever asked the larrens down here?"

"No. Look, we normally don't tell kids about this until they're older, but I think you should know. Do you remember hearing up on the mesa that nineteen out of twenty jumpers made it?"

"Yeah."

"And how did we know that?"

"They would light signal fires."

"Right. Well, it turns out that only about fifteen out of twenty actually survive. If the jumpers manage to come down near a town almost everyone survives, but of the ones who land in the forest only about half survive. So, who lights the signal fires for the missing four? We don't know for sure, but we think it must be the larrens. They deny it, but who else could it be? And what possible reason could they have for doing it? Why would they want people on the mesa to think more people survive? So you can understand why most of us are cautious about the larrens. We don't think we can trust them. We've talked about how the larrens keep their distance from us, but that's a big part of why we keep our distance from them."

"I think Wilton was lying to me. I know everyone else thinks so. I've thought he lied to me for a long time now, but it makes me feel so stupid when I think about it. I never wanted to admit it or talk about it."

"Kraster, you were ten!"

"Do you think he was lying?"

"He admitted it to me. It was one of the last things he said. I was furious. I probably should have told you, but, I suppose I thought it might be easier not to know."

"It's okay. I get so angry too, but then my embarrassment at being tricked - that's even worse. The reason I brought it up is that I think I know what I should do, but the last big decision I made was a disaster. I wanted to bring you up here and talk it through."

"Okay, let's talk it through."

Kraster's face grew serious as he lined up his thoughts. "I left my family on the mesa and I want to get back to them. More than anything. I promised Myree I would try to find a way up. It was the last thing I told her. As soon as she turns sixteen, she's going to find a larren and make the jump; I'm almost sure of it. She'll leave Mom and Dad to try to come find me, all because I was dumb enough to believe a ridiculous story. If I can find a way back up there, I can keep her from making the jump. I can put our family back together."

"If you try going around the mesa and never come back, then Myree will make the jump in a few years and you won't be here for her. She'd be alone. Actually, she would probably follow you and try to go around the mesa too. Besides, I remember you telling me that she wouldn't jump because she thought you were dead."

"I used to think that, but you don't know Myree. She's really… I don't want to make her sound bad, but she's really stubborn. If she isn't sure I'm dead, I think she'll try to come down."

"Maybe she's changed. She was only eight when you jumped."

"It's possible. Has my personality changed a lot since then?"

"No, I suppose not."

"Anyway, I think she'll try. Is it possible the people that go around find a route up and that's why they don't come back?"

"No, think about it. If that was true, we would have heard about it when we were up on the mesa. Everyone would know that there was a way up the cliffs on the other side."

"Yeah, I guess you're right. How many people have wandered off trying to go around since you've been down here?"

"Not many, I can only think of one actually. Ranis left about ten years ago."

"Was she a really good climber?"

"Average from what I hear. She just hated not knowing what was on the other side. She said she would hike straight around and come right back, no climbing or anything. She wanted to prove there was nothing to be afraid of, and then when she didn't come back it just made everyone more afraid."

"I hate this! What do you think I should do?"

Cindl didn't want to answer. She wanted him to stay close where she could protect him, but he was fifteen. Hardly any boy left. "Kraster, I don't want you to go, but I'll support your decision either way. I don't know what I'd do if I was in your shoes."

"If Myree comes down and I'm not here, will you take care of her for me?"

"If your sixteen-year-old sister will accept any help from me, then I'll be happy to."

"I think I have to try. I'm going to try. I hope I'm making the right decision."

CHAPTER SEVEN
BONES

It was hard to wait after making the decision to go, but Kraster stuck around until the end of September to make sure almost all the harvesting was done. There would be more to do over the next month, but the hardest work was behind them and Cindl told him he could go. Cindl helped him pack and she handled the goodbye better than he expected.

His trek took him southeast along the base of the cliffs. Echo Canyon was a natural barrier that defined the eastern edge of their territory and it took him two days to get across. Climbing down one side and up the other had been easy; it was the river itself that was difficult. It was the same river that formed a boundary on the mesa and it flowed fast and deep in most places. He spent a whole day looking for a shallow crossing or a very wide section with a slower current. In the end, he picked a spot with an island in the middle so he could at least split the swim in half. Once across the canyon he was immediately rewarded with views of the cliffs he'd never seen before. Sometimes he could hike right along the base of the cliffs and they towered up over him, but most of the time the terrain forced him to make long detours out away from the cliffs.

He was on the best climbing route he'd found so far. He wasn't sure, but there were several places where he thought the handholds had been smoothed just a bit. On the common routes back near Lin the best handholds were always smooth from so many hands polishing away the rough edges. The smoothing here was so faint he wondered if it was his imagination. It was a very easy climb. His friends would have called it a toddler route. He looked down and realized that this was the highest he'd ever climbed! The route started to veer to the right and ended at a three-meter gap where the cliff face curved inward and was almost completely smooth. There was one small foothold about half way across and he knew from experience that with a one-step approach he could jump and plant his left foot on that ledge and then make the second jump to the other side. The trick would be getting back. The ledge on the other side of the gap was a little below his current position and making the jumps coming back would be difficult. He'd made similar jumps in the past, but this was taking a bit more risk than he would like. From the ledge on the other side, the route appeared to continue upward to the right.

Kraster leaned back to get the momentum he needed, jumped to the small ledge, and then powered off the foothold to land easily on the other side. Without even looking back to think about the return, he started following the route upward.

Five minutes later he was on a long narrow ledge that cut into the cliff face, and at the far end was a human skull and a pile of bones. He felt his whole body tense and freeze, but a second later his heart was pounding in his chest. A real skeleton. He'd never seen one before, just pictures. He moved closer, trying to walk silently without realizing it. Unlike the neat pictures at school, most of the bones were not connected anymore. That made it hard to imagine how tall the person must have been, but as he examined the bones and skull, it became obvious that this had been a small person. From the way the bones were lying, he guessed that she had died sitting with her back in the small nook just to the right of where the bones now lay. Was she really a girl? Some wisps of long hair made him think so, but he wasn't sure. As his heart rate slowed, he studied the bones with more care. He compared his hand to the bones on the ground trying to confirm his suspicion that she had been very young - maybe ten or eleven?

Under her jaw, he thought he could see some metal. It took several minutes to work up the courage to touch the bones, but then he gently moved her skull and picked up a copper square with a hole punched in one corner. It looked like the copper had been pounded into flat sheets and roughly cut into squares. It wasn't even a perfect square and the cuts were not straight lines. This was not jewelry. Based on where he found it, he guessed it must have been carried around her neck on a string which had long since rotted away. One side was covered in symbols he'd never seen before. It looked like writing, with neat rows and a few repeated symbols, but he couldn't make anything of it. He pulled some string from his pack, pulled it through the hole, tied it off and pulled it over his head. Whoever she was, she deserved to be remembered.

After scouring the ledge for ten minutes, he couldn't find any way to proceed and realized the dead girl must have come to the same conclusion. And she must not have thought she could make the jump back either.

"Goodbye. I hate just leaving you here, but I guess you've

been here a really long time already. If you were a ten-year-old girl, then I'm really impressed you made that jump back there. But I don't understand why you're here. When I get back home, I'll show this around and try to figure out who you are. Maybe I can find your family. I hate thinking of you sitting up here by yourself dying. Why would you be up here by yourself? Did whoever was with you fall? But you're not alone anymore. I know about you. I know where you are and I won't forget about you."

I was hard to turn his back on her, but Kraster made his way back to the gap and paused to imagine how it must have looked to a young girl; maybe to someone like Myree. Then he lunged across the way he came, using the small foothold in the middle and climbed back down to the forest.

CHAPTER EIGHT

FOLLOWED

KRASTER WOKE UP crying the next morning. In his dreams, the girl on the ledge was Myree. She was scared and alone and none of his efforts would change anything. He was embarrassed and glanced around to make sure he was alone. It was silly, but the whole thing had him on edge, so he skipped breakfast and packed up quickly. Walking felt good but his mind was distracted and he almost missed the small piece of paper wedged into the bark of a small tree along his path with a large letter "K" visible. He unfolded the note, read it quickly and put it in his pocket.

- K,Climb at the next Gisenda tree. C -

The was no mistaking which tree she meant, and although the route didn't look promising, he left his heavy pack in the shade, tightened his climbing pack, and started up the cliff. After only a couple minutes of climbing he saw Cindl resting at the mouth of a large cave opening.

Before he could say anything, she signaled for him to be quiet and motioned for him to follow her higher up the cliff. They climbed up around the left side of the cave and kept going for another ten minutes before they found a good place to stop. Cindl gave Kraster a hug so tight it hurt.

"I'm so glad you're okay! There are five larrens following you and I'm worried they plan to hurt you; maybe even kill you."

"What? Why? Why would they want to kill me?"

"I don't know, but I can't think of any good reason why they'd be following you. And I can't help wonder if everyone who tries to go around the mesa gets followed. Maybe that's why they never come back."

"You were following me?"

"I'm sorry Kraster. I promised myself a long time ago that I was going to look out for you. You look mad."

"Well, maybe a little. Give me a second. This is a lot to absorb in ten seconds." Kraster leaned against the rocks and looked back down toward the forest. "I can't imagine why they'd be following me either. What should we do?"

"I don't know yet, but I needed to let you know what was happening so you'd be ready if they attack. I'll keep following, but honestly, I'm not sure what we could really do if they attack."

"Maybe we can lose them. If they don't know that I know, we should be able to slip away. Maybe in the middle of the night?"

"I haven't watched them all night, but I've watched them a little and they've always had one larren watching you while you sleep."

"We need a climbing route that lets us double back behind them. You know, where you can climb up one route and come down another."

"That's a really great idea. I'll try to scout for a route up ahead and I'll leave you another note. So take your time and try lots of routes - just to give me time. If they come at you, scream and I'll come help as fast as I can."

Cindl's last comment brought the weight of their situation crashing down. "Okay, and you scream if they come after you."

Cindl tried to smile. "I will. You'd better get back down before they wonder what's taking so long. Act normal."

"Oh, I almost forgot, look at this. I found it on a skeleton really high up the cliffs yesterday."

"A skeleton?"

"Yeah. Well, a pile of bones. It looked like a little girl's skeleton. It might have been a boy; definitely a kid though. I think this must have been around her neck. Can you read it?"

"No, I've never seen anything like this! It's strange. It doesn't look ornamental."

"I know; it's really roughly made. Maybe a prayer or a blessing of some sort?"

"That could be, but why write a prayer with coded symbols?

"You think it's a code?"

"Just a guess. It's definitely not any writing I've ever seen. Either way, people usually take a lot of care making prayers or blessings beautiful. Hold on to this. We'll ask around when we get back to see if anyone recognizes the writing."

Kraster climbed back down first, picked up his pack and moved on along the base of the cliffs. Thirty minutes later, Cindl raced down the final stretch of the route that was visible from the ground and disappeared into the trees.

CHAPTER NINE
THE WORST SLAVE

THE NEXT TWO days passed slowly. There were no notes from Cindl and Kraster started to wonder what was going on. He was staying close to the cliff face which meant a lot of climbing in and out of ravines and over boulder fields. He could have gone around most of them, but he didn't want to miss any notes from Cindl. And, the larrens must hate this. Larrens were decent climbers in their youth, but they were horrible climbers as they grew older. It was fun to imagine them having to take the long way around the steepest parts and running to keep up with him.

It was getting late in the afternoon and he decided to set up camp before the sun got much lower. He built a small fire that would make a perfect bed of coals in about half an hour. After everything was in order, Kraster picked one of the tree trunks upwind from his fire and sat down against it. The copper message plate around his neck jabbed his chest and he pulled it off to look at it again. He held it up into the firelight but the symbols remained a mystery.

"Where'd you get that?" Kraster jumped to his feet and

turned to face the unexpected voice. "I asked you a question and if you know what's good for you, you'll answer me right now."

"What do you care? Besides, who are you?"

"Doesn't matter who I am. I was about to kill you until I saw the message plate. I still might. Where'd you get it?"

"On the cliffs. I guess I don't care if you know where I got it. I found it with the bones of a little girl. What is it?" Kraster tried to keep his voice calm but his palms were sweating and he'd never been more afraid.

"Again, doesn't matter. I'm taking you to King Marik. He'll decide what to do about you and that message."

"King Marik? Never heard of him. I'm going around the mesa and I didn't ask for your permission."

The large larren seemed genuinely amused. "Look kid, you're surrounded so don't think you can get away. Besides, the King might give you a reward or something. Those are pretty rare! Let's go."

There was a scuffle behind Kraster and he turned to see Cindl attacking a larren on the other side of his fire. He screamed and sprinted into the fight, but they were no match for the larren. Three other larrens emerged from their hiding places but stood back to let their friend gradually wear the humans down.

"Tie 'em up!"

"Both of them? Shouldn't we kill the woman?"

"No, let's bring her too. They obviously know each other so she might have information about the message. Besides, she looks strong for a human. Probably make a good slave."

The next three days were brutal. The larrens looked for ways to make the trip miserable. No food at all, they were only allowed to get a drink once a day, and the youngest larren never tired of throwing rocks and large branches at them. By the time they reached the outskirts of Rreker they were exhausted and beaten, but the sight of the larren city shocked them to attention. It was larger than anything they'd ever seen on the mesa and it made Lin look tiny. They entered through a large gate that cut through the five-meter-high walls. The streets were wide, with larrens and a few humans moving in both directions. No one paid any attention to them as they made their way toward the palace complex at the center of Rreker.

At the heart of the city was a large open circle that was carefully paved with broad streets branching out in every direction. Around the circle were all the most important buildings in Rreker. The palace was the largest and looked the newest. Beside the palace was the King's Guard's Barracks, which had once been an actual barracks, but was now the headquarters for the King's Guard. Directly across the circle from the palace was the Council Building where all the smartest larrens debated and studied. Filling in the two arcs around the circle were the Grand Library, several museums, the Human Theatre where human slaves put on elaborate shows, and dozens of smaller less important buildings. The circle itself appeared to be in complete chaos at first glance. People and larrens moved in every conceivable direction with street vendors and musicians scattered throughout. But as they neared the center, they started to see the order hidden in the chaos. Although there were no marked paths, everyone flowed through invisible channels that crisscrossing the circle and connected all the streets together. Along those pathways were the vendors and performers. Despite all the activity, the circle felt sparse. Either it was too big, or there weren't enough larrens to fill it.

Cindl and Kraster were dragged through the outer sections of the palace and thrown to the floor in front of King Marik. He was resting on a large red cushion in the middle of the room with a pile of empty plates beside him. A human slave was just entering the room through a different door and collected the plates. Kraster kept trying to make eye contact, but she kept her eyes down and moved fast. The room was framed by a circle of columns made of bluish gray stone. The columns were as tall as trees and sunlight filtered down from unseen openings high above them. He was just noticing the paintings on the wall beyond the columns when his attention was drawn back the King.

"King Marik! Our guards found these two humans exploring along the cliff face and brought them here. Normally they would have been killed, but the boy had an old war message and they thought you would want to know about it."

"Excellent judgement. Give those guards a month holiday and one slave each. Have the humans brought closer." Kraster and Cindl were pushed from behind so hard and suddenly that Cindl stumbled and fell.

"What's wrong with you!" Kraster glared at the guards as he helped Cindl to her feet. She was weak from their ordeal but fought not to show it. "If you want us to move forward, just ask!"

"One strike for the boy."

As soon as the King spoke, the guard closest to them stepped forward and struck Kraster so hard it sent him sprawling across the floor. Pain shot through his right arm as he tried to push himself back up. It felt like it might be broken and a new fierce anger flooded his mind.

But the King spoke before Kraster could. "Now, tell me

how you came to possess an old war message or the woman gets two strikes."

Kraster's mind raced through his options, but he clenched his jaw and forced his anger into the background. He would not allow Cindl to be hurt if there was anything he could do about it.

"I was climbing the cliffs looking for a route up and I came to a spot with a difficult jump. On the other side there was a skeleton of what I think was a young girl. I found the message among her bones. I assume it was hung around her neck. And my name is Kraster since you didn't ask."

"One strike for the woman." Cindl was ready and absorbed the blow without falling but she ended up several paces from where she started. She was trying not to show it, but it was obvious she was in pain. "You were doing so well at first. I don't care what your name is. Answer the question I ask you. Have you ever seen something like this before?"

"No." The battle in Kraster's mind was unlike anything he had ever faced. His anger demanded action and revenge while his logic demanded obedience for Cindl's sake.

"See, that was perfect. I guess stupid humans can learn a little. Can you read the inscription?"

"No."

"Do you have any idea why a girl would be carrying this inscription while climbing the cliffs?"

"No."

"And were you born on the mesa or the base?"

"On the mesa, I came down about five years ago."

"Very well. It appears the mesa humans remain ignorant of their past." He turned to his guards, "you may remove the humans".

"Sir, what would you like us to do with them?"

The King looked them over quietly with just the faintest trace of a smile then focused on Kraster. "I can't give this young man to anyone I know. He'd be about the worst slave imaginable. Is the tunnel still asking for more help?"

"Yes Sir. They've been struggling to keep up the pace."

"Well, that settles it. I think these two would be perfect in the tunnel."

CHAPTER TEN

LOST HOUSES

IT WAS EXACTLY one month since Myree celebrated the five-year anniversary of Kraster's jump. Celebrate wasn't really the right word for it, especially since it was mostly in secret. Her family went through the normal charade. At supper they each took turns saying something they remembered about Kraster. It was a charade because none of them would say what they really thought. She still acted like she thought he was dead and planned out the memory she would share weeks in advance. And she couldn't imagine that her parents were sure he was dead, but neither side wanted to be the first to break the pattern. She hated the whole thing. For one thing, she was thirteen, sneaking up on fourteen, and her parents had to know she wasn't sure Kraster was dead. Maybe they could have believed it for the first few years, but now it bordered on insulting. At some point they would have to talk about the real Kraster, not the pretend Kraster who was definitely dead. The thought of just blurting out the truth was so tempting, but she didn't know what they would do. They could clamp down tighter. No, she'd decided that her parents would have to admit they were pretending first. They started it.

Sometimes she'd imagine sitting with her Mom and having a real conversation about Kraster. She needed one so badly. Her initial grief had faded, but she still thought about him often. It was mostly the good memories now, but the old question had lingered and solidified in her mind as she asked it over and over. There was no escape from it; she hadn't tried to stop Kraster. She could have cried and clung to him. Maybe she could have run for help, yelling for attention as she went. Maybe just asking him not to go would have been enough. But she had just given him a last hug. He had slow-punched her cheek like he always did back then and scuffed up her hair which he knew she hated. Then, she just watched him go. Her parents had never blamed her; they had never come out and accused her directly, but she felt the weight of her guilt in their sadness. She knew it wasn't all her fault, but her share of it had become a familiar and heavy burden. Partly because of her, Kraster was either dead or alone down below.

Kraster wouldn't recognize the mesa anymore. Larrens were a rare sight; no one had larren friends anymore. Right around her last birthday, she'd seen a larren being escorted through the center circle, probably on the way to some important meeting. She caught herself staring, and then noticed that all the kids were staring, as were most of the adults. But the walls were still up. In fact, it was worse now. Once the first wall was finished, more were built further out to enclose some of the nearby farms until most of the land around town was a honeycomb of walls. Not that it mattered. She was the only thirteen-year-old she knew of who wasn't even allowed outside the first wall. It was admittedly a very large cage, but she hadn't left town since the jump.

It was a cool early autumn morning and Myree walked toward home. She felt sick earlier that morning and her teacher sent her to see the nurse who promptly sent her home for the day. Her classmates liked to joke that the nurse was a fraud because almost everyone who went to see her was sent home, but Myree thought she might just be lazy. By the time she walked out the school door, she was already feeling a lot better, but she decided to keep that to herself and enjoy a day off. It wasn't that she didn't like school; she did. Her grades were always good, but like so many other things, she suspected the teachers went a bit easy on her. Most adults, and even many of the other kids her age, handled her with care - like she might break. That might have been true a few years ago, but not anymore. She wasn't fragile.

It was perfect walking weather and she decided she didn't feel like going home yet. She turned toward the center circle and Korel's store. Korel sold clothing and household goods, but much more important to Myree, her store was also the unofficial hub for the small group of writers on the mesa. If anyone wrote a story, they would bring a copy to Korel's. Korel used her downtime to read them and make copies. People could check out a story for ten bits, but the tradition was to write out a second copy if you enjoyed it and bring it back to Korel's with the original. Myree always made two copies so she could keep one for herself and her collection of twenty-six stories was her most valued possession.

"Hey Korel!" The shop was empty as she'd hoped it would be.

"Myree! So good to see you. Can I assume you're sick today?"

Korel knew all about the school nurse and they both smiled at the joke. "Oh, I can hardly stand! You know, she'd make a great story character. Maybe I'll finally get up the courage to try writing my own story for you."

"You should. I'd love to read it."

Myree walked to the shelves where the stories were kept and started looking through them for something interesting. "I'm just kidding. I'm too scared to let people see what I'm thinking. Do you have any new ones you think I'd like?"

"I just got a couple last week but I haven't finished copying them yet. One of them is really good; I think you'll like it. I'll have it done by tomorrow if you want to swing by. Should I hold if for you?"

"Sure. I can't wait!" Korel almost always recommended great stories and Myree had stopped asking what they were about. It was more fun to just read them and find out. But she wouldn't get it until tomorrow and she still had most of a day left. "You need any help in the store today? I'm not quite ready to go home."

"No. I don't think so. It's been slow recently so I'm caught up on my side projects. Thanks for offering."

"Sure. Maybe I'll work on making a copy. Do you mind if I hang out back here and work on one?"

Korel had her mischievous grin on. "No I don't mind, but I have an idea for you. If you're interested."

"I should be nervous, shouldn't I?"

"I was talking to my Dad yesterday and he claims there's a hidden street on the far southern edge of town. Right along the drop."

"Really? I thought it was just old storage buildings down there."

"Me too, but I guess it's the oldest part of town and there used to be houses along the drop. I'd heard that before, but my Dad claims there was a short row of old houses that ended up penned in by buildings and they just walled it off instead of tearing them down. Anyway, I'm dying to know if it's still there. You could go check it out for me."

"How am I supposed to find them?"

"I don't know. I haven't thought about the details. Look, only if you want to. I thought it sounded fun, but I don't want to pressure you. Besides, I'm skeptical about the whole story. I've lived here my whole life and talk to customers every day and I'd never heard of this until yesterday."

"I'm just a little nervous, that's all. I think I'd like to go. Did he give you any clues about where it might be?"

"No, he'd never seen it. We were talking about a story we just read and something about it reminded him of the houses. He claims his grandfather told him the story when he was a kid. He'd forgotten about it."

"I hope it's real. If it is, I'm getting my family to move there. Then, when someone asks where I live, I can say it's a secret. Alright, I'll go. If I get in trouble for snooping around, I'll blame you."

"That sounds fair."

They said goodbye and Myree headed south. As she walked, her nervousness grew. She couldn't think of a reason why she shouldn't be looking for the houses, but it felt like a secret mission. That was it. She always thought of Kraster when she thought of secret missions, and that example was full of failure and consequences. Being on a secret mission of any sort was like hearing echoes of those failures and sorrows in her mind. She almost turned around, but she'd told Korel she would go.

The south end of town was built along the edge of a long rock cliff. It wasn't the main cliff that defined the mesa itself, but a smaller cliff on top of the mesa where one hard layer of rock had eroded away revealing the next layer or rock below it. Everyone called it the drop to avoid confusion. It was only about ten meters high, but it was enough to form a natural boundary on two sides of town. As time passed and the population grew, things had shifted in the directions they could. And long before Myree's grandparents were born this had become the old run-down part of town, and then it had stopped being a place anyone lived. There were still a lot of nice houses along the drop, but they were further east where it curved north and faced the river.

The streets were a maze and she kept having to stop and find the sun to make sure she was still heading south. In fifteen minutes she had emerged on a long gently curving street that ran east-west. All the other streets appeared to end at this street and she decided it must run parallel to the drop. It was a guess because the south side of the street was blocked off by a row of very old buildings, almost all of which appeared to be abandoned. There was no one around and she had the urge to hide, but she forced herself to walk casually down the street, looking for any clue that one of the buildings might hide her goal. Nothing stood out. She couldn't tell how far back they went and there were no gaps between the buildings. The solution was simple, but she wished she didn't have to go alone. She needed to find a way to climb up on one of the roofs.

There were no obvious ways to climb up the fronts, and

besides, she was sure someone would come around a corner and yell at her to get down. She backtracked along the street looking for a way into one of the abandoned buildings and finally found a door that might work. Like most of the doorways she'd passed, this one had boards nailed across it at various angles, but a few had fallen off and she knew she could step through the gap without too much trouble. Behind the boards, the door hung loosely on its hinges and there was no lock she could see. It was the middle of the day, so she couldn't sneak in. She just had to hope no one was watching. As quickly as she could, she approached the door and reached through the boards to test it. It swung open easily enough, and with a quick glance back down the street, she stepped between the boards, through the doorway and pulled it closed behind her. She couldn't see anything and her heart was racing faster than she'd realized. With her hands held out in front, she took several steps further in to get away from the door. The floor felt like dirt under her shoes, with gravel and unseen debris. Slowly, her eyes started to pick up more details. She was in a large room with two other doorways; one to the side and one leading further back. The stone walls had been carefully plastered to a smooth finish, but it was impossible to tell in the low light what color they had been. She didn't dare force a window open to find out. There was nothing else in the room. Any furniture had been removed long ago.

Myree walked carefully through the doorway that led further back into the building and immediately had to turn right or left down a long hallway. She picked right and felt her way deeper into the darkness. She moved slowly, moving back and forth between the two walls looking for another doorway. Finally, on the left side of the hallway, she felt a door frame and a closed door. She pushed on the handle but it wouldn't budge. She pulled and felt a little give, but it still wouldn't open. Myree ran her fingers up and down along the edge trying to find a latch or lock that might be holding it closed, but there was nothing. It was hard to tell in the dark, but if felt like the bottom of the door was catching more than the top. Squatting down, she ran her fingers along the floor and found what she was looking for. It was nothing but a board laid down on the floor across the hallway; one end against the door and the other against the opposite wall. If there was any light it would be the worst lock imaginable, but in almost total darkness it had almost worked. With the board out of the way, the door swung open quietly and she stepped into what was clearly the main room.

It was much larger than the front room and used up most of the building. At the opposite end of the room a shaft of sunlight came through a hole in the ceiling and lit up a column of dust hanging in the air. Everything was so still, so quiet. Filling the space between her and the column of light was a maze of old animal stalls, with narrow passageways winding their way through. Every stall could have a person hidden inside. The thought had popped into her head and there was no way to get it out. After all, it was silly to think she was the only person that had decided to explore this building. If someone was in here, they would have heard her coming down the hallway. But she would probably be able to hear them too if they moved at all. She stood perfectly still and waited; listening for anything. The dust in the light began to move. Still very slowly, but more than before. Could she be causing that just by entering the room? Or maybe it was from the hole in the ceiling. She didn't know. But if it was because of her, then that was a good sign.

Someone else moving around in here before her should have had the same effect, but the dust had looked almost still when she first came in. She could feel the fear rising in her stomach but she was as scared to go back down the dark hallway as she was to move toward the light.

She moved to the first stall and quickly glanced over the side. Empty. She moved in further, checking the stall on either side of her as she walked.

"You can come out." Myree's voice was much louder than she expected. Then more quietly, "I can hear you breathing." She looked around the room to see if her ploy had worked and hoping desperately that there was no one to trick.

The room returned to total silence and she resumed her slow winding path across the room. Her ears hummed as they struggled to pick up the smallest scratch or creak. But nothing happened and soon she was standing beside the shaft of light looking up at the hole. It was easily big enough to climb through if she could pull herself up through it. One of the stall walls was almost directly below the opening and she climbed up and balanced at a corner so she could stand up. Leading up to the hole, someone had put in ladder rungs among the rafters. They weren't exactly hidden, but she hadn't noticed them before. This was exactly what she had hoped to find, but it confirmed the obvious - other people came here. She imagined someone sneaking up behind her. This was silly! There wasn't anyone there and she couldn't let every little imagined fear control her. But the impulse was too strong; she turned to look just to be sure. No one.

If she jumped she should be able to grab the first rung. The question was whether she was strong enough to pull herself up to the second one. If she couldn't, the drop to the floor might hurt, but it wasn't high enough to kill her. The worst case scenario was that she might break her ankle or leg on the landing.

The enormity of her little adventure suddenly came into focus. How had she let herself get this far? She was alone in a dark abandoned building, balancing on a wall and preparing to make a jump that might result in a broken leg. She had never done anything like this! But to stop now seemed impossible. The answer to her question was up through that opening, so she jumped and grabbed the bottom rung. She waited just long enough for her body to stop swinging and then pulled herself up with all her strength. Her chin crept up until it was above her hands and she looked up at the next rung. Keeping her left hand on the first rung, she jerked her right hand up and grabbed the second. She'd made a mistake, she needed to pull herself up one more rung before she could catch anything with her foot. A shiver of fear moved through her at the thought of failure. Her arms were already shaking but she pulled herself upward again, her legs kicking violently underneath her. But she had it! Her hands were starting to really hurt - she couldn't stop to rest. After a few attempts, she caught a rafter with her foot and used the extra leverage to pull herself up another rung, and then she could get her knee on the first rung. She had done it. She climbed the last two rungs and rolled out onto the roof, completely exhausted and very proud.

Her body wanted to rest, but her mind raced. She rolled on to her belly but stayed low against the roof. Below her, the mesa spread out to the south and in a few places she could see the desert horizon. To her left was the river valley that cut across the center of the mesa. She couldn't see the river, but she could see the trees and she remembered the sound of the running water; the surprise and joy of the cold water. Toward the edge of the mesa the river had cut a deep gorge as it cascaded down to the base. She remembered Kraster telling her that someday the river would cut the mesa in half. It was a good memory and it made her smile. The wind was blowing toward the river but she wondered if she would be able to hear the falls if it were blowing the other direction.

Beyond the river was larren territory. It was so close, but it might as well be across the desert. Off to her right, the mesa became gradually more stark and barren, with wind-swept trees and grasses replacing the fields and pastures closer to town.

It was time to get moving. One of the farmers below was sure to look up and see her if she stood and walked, and if anyone was in a building below her, they might hear her on the roof. She would have to crawl quietly. Moving so slowly was irritating, but she wouldn't let her impatience ruin this whole trip. She was getting hungry and thirsty, and was starting to get warm in her jacket with the sun's never-ending press and the surprisingly tiring work of slow, deliberate movement. But then she saw it, a gap in the roofs! She was halfway across the third building from where she started and there was a gap between the third and fourth buildings. She sped up and tried to compensate by working even harder at being quiet.

It was narrower than she had expected, but below her were normal houses. Rather than a row of houses along the edge of the cliff as she had been imagining, it was a row of houses coming in from the cliffs. There were four houses and then, closest to the cliff, what looked like another stable and it struck her that this was incredibly important. From the fields below, it would just look like another small storage building. If any of the houses had been at the edge, everyone would know about this place.

There was no street in front of the houses - that part of the story was wrong. The other buildings had been built right up against the old houses. For such old houses, the roofs were in surprisingly good shape. Someone was taking care of them. So she wasn't surprised to find the ladder that dropped down between the two middle houses. Did someone live here or was it a just a kind of clubhouse - a secret place to escape? As she had in the first building, she waited for several minutes at the edge listening for any sound. Then she dropped her legs over the edge until they touched the ladder and carefully climbed down into the shadows. It was tempting to yell hello, but instinctively she knew to be quiet. A place like this wouldn't be a secret if the people who came yelled at each other. As if to confirm her thoughts, a sign was posted on the wall opposite from the ladder. "Please keep this secret". For the first time, she hoped someone was there. Someone she could share this with.

Between the two houses at the bottom of the ladder was a clear packed-dirt path with patches of garden plants and a few tired flowers on either side. It didn't seem like there would be enough sunlight to have a proper garden, but someone had tried it anyway. Along the front of the houses, there was enough room to walk and she decided to explore the house farthest from the drop first. There were minor differences, but they were all very small, with stone walls, small openings for windows, a fireplace in the middle, hooks along the tops of the walls to hang up thick curtains in winter, and carefully laid flagstone floors. Each house was clean and taken care of to some degree, but the fourth house, the one closest to the cliffs, was clearly the focus. It seemed early, but dark blue winter curtains draped the walls. Maybe they used them to muffle sound. There was a table, two desks, chairs, piles of crates along one wall, and even four bedrolls. The ashes in the fireplace were cold, but it must get occasional use. In the kitchen she found a jug of water and helped herself to a drink. There was a surprising amount of food as well, but taking some without permission felt different than taking a drink and she left it alone.

Last she came to the building she had assumed was a stable. Once inside she could tell it had probably been a workshop of some kind. Maybe a carpenter's. The back wall was typical stonework, but it had a small open window that looked out over the cliff. It probably wouldn't raise any alarms if a farmer saw her looking out a window, but she still stayed several steps back in the shadows. On the floor, near the corner of the room, someone had thrown a blanket over a pile. That alone would not have been noteworthy, but she could see a faint sliver of light between the edge of the blanket and the wall. Other than the water jug, she still hadn't touched anything, but why would there be light coming from the floor? She pulled the blanket away revealing a hole that dropped straight down. A large crack ran up the cliff from the bottom all the way to the top, where it undermined the shop's outer wall and a section of the floor. Now that she knew to look for it, she could see that the stones in the remaining floor had spread apart a little where the crack must be slowly widening underneath. If it continued, it would eventually start to damage the row of houses. And now it all made sense, why people hundreds of years ago had decided to leave these houses alone rather than tear them down and build a new storehouse in their place.

Someone had used old lumber to cover the hole, some laid

across it and some propped up at an angle to the wall, and then covered it all with the blanket. It didn't seem like a trap, but she could imagine someone falling through. As Myree looked down the crack, her breath caught in her throat. If she could climb down and back up the crack, she would have a way to leave town for the first time in five years! The rock looked rough enough to provide handholds, and she thought she could even press her back against one side and her feet and hands against the other. Even better, the crack was deep enough that she thought she would be able to climb it without being seen by a farmer in the fields. She would have to be very careful about that.

It was so tempting but she couldn't try it today. Her arms were too tired and if she couldn't get back up she would have to explain how she got out. She moved the lumber back into place and covered the hole with the blanket. She would be back, and next time she would bring a rope.

CHAPTER ELEVEN

NATIVES

THE TUNNEL SLAVE camp was a small village, very tightly packed with several rings of fences surrounding it and larrens patrolling between the fences at all times. One edge was about 200 meters from the base of the cliff and there was a fenced corridor connecting the camp to the tunnel entrance. Originally, the camp had been laid out in a normal hub and spoke pattern by the larrens, with wide straight roads crossing it to allow for the larren guards to patrol among the shelters. That was hundreds of years ago. As more slaves were thrown into the camp, the living quarters became more densely packed. The small passageways between shacks were only large enough for one human at a time and the larren guards gradually stopped patrolling larger and larger sections of the camp. Piece by piece, even the radial streets from the central hub were filled in with makeshift homes and shops. The larrens never came into camp anymore. There was only one open space left. At the very center of camp, the humans had kept the central plaza open. It was a place where people gathered to mingle, where meetings were held and where the shifts competed against each other during the Rain Games.

Kraster and Cindl stood at the last gate before entering the camp. As dirty and chaotic as it looked, Kraster couldn't wait to get away from the larrens and rejoin his fellow humans. One guard opened the gate while the guard behind shoved them through. A tall big-boned man was waiting for them inside. The first thing Kraster noticed were the muscles in his forearm when he extended his hand in welcome. They rippled under his skin and although he didn't squeeze too hard, it was obvious he could crush Kraster's bones if he felt like it. He was intimidating and happy at the same time. Kraster liked him immediately.

"Welcome to Camp! The names Jenik. And who might you two be?"

"I'm Cindl and this is Kraster."

"It's a pleasure to meet you both! So how'd you end up getting thrown in here anyway?"

Cindl glanced at Kraster to let him answer. "I was trying to go around the mesa to look for a climbing route to the top but we were captured by larrens and sent here."

"Really! Well that's unusual. You two might be the only ones in fact. Can't think of anyone else. Usually, the newbies are just slaves that can't seem to stay out of trouble! Their owners finally just give up and throw em in here. I guess King Marik considers it a favor when larrens donate slaves to the tunnels. Still, usually only happens as a last resort. Well, anyway, you're about to be celebrities of a sort, coming from the Free Lands and all. So what's it like over there?"

Kraster and Cindl took turns talking about Lin, their farm, the fringe, the other human villages, and the mesa as Jenik led them deeper into the camp. Everything they said seemed to amaze him and Kraster caught himself laughing for the first time in over a week.

"You said your name was Krasser?"

"No, Kraster."

"Got it, got it. So, we're almost there. Don't worry about finding your way back yet. It's a maze at first, no question. I'll tell your shift leader where you've been assigned and he'll make sure you get back here alright. And in a week, you'll know this place like the back of your hand! And it was Cindl, right?"

"That's right."

"There's a section in Ring One that's for women only, but they thought you'd want to keep an eye on your son. I know I would! But just thought you should know about it in case you want to move over there in a few years once your boy's grown up a bit."

Kraster felt Cindl squeeze his arm and knew to let the misunderstanding slide.

"Thanks, maybe in a couple years. So, when's our first shift?"

"You're in 2nd Shift, so let's see, you guys head up in two days, at sunrise. It'll take you about seventeen hours to hike up to the dig zone, then you'll work until the Third Shift relieves you."

"And a new shift leaves camp every two days?"

"That's right. So basically, you march up there and dig for two days, then the next shift shows up and you march back down. There's four shifts all together."

Kraster was trying to piece the schedule together in his mind. "Where will we sleep while we're in the tunnel?"

"Ha! You won't sleep much at all. They'll throw as much

food at you as you want, but you'll be lucky if you can grab a couple hours of sleep. The whole point of this operation is to have humans digging all the time. Actually, I forgot Krasser, they made you a creeper! You can probably get some sleep! Especially with all the caves in the section we're digging now. I doubt you'll do much digging on this shift. Two hasn't had a creeper in over a month; since what's-his-name died. I should know his name. Ah well, I didn't really know the guy. Kind of kept to himself. Anyway, my point being, if you wanted to nap in one of those caves, I don't see how they could stop you!"

"I've never stayed awake for two days."

"Now don't get mad at me Krasser, it's a bit over three days if you include the trip up and down on either side of the digging. But you get used to it. You'll always hate it, but I guess you just accept it after a while. You'll sleep for a whole day when you get back. Then you'll wake up for five or six hours and then go back to bed. Usually you're rested enough that you can enjoy the last two or three days before your next shift."

"Hey, Jenik, can I ask a basic question?"

"I've been told all my questions are basic. Fire away!"

"I guess I'm still trying to understand… what's the tunnel for exactly?"

Jenik seemed unsure how to answer this. "Well, the tunnel would allow humans and larrens to move back and forth between the mesa and the base."

"I know that. But it's so much work. It doesn't seem worth it."

"Ah! I see what you mean. I suppose you'd have to ask the King himself to know for sure. I've always thought he just hates how the larrens and humans seem to get along on the mesa. Doesn't seem right to him and he'd love to control the mesa too. Well, here we are! Number 412. If you get lost, you are Second Shift, Ring 3, number 412. Anyone who's been here more than a few weeks will be able to help you get back. Now I'll leave you to get settled and feel free to track me down if you need anything."

Cindl made a small bow of appreciation. "Thank you for showing us to our home."

"Ma'am, no one calls 'em homes! We call 'em shacks, but you're welcome just the same! Oh, and one last thing you should know; the larrens will let you out if you provide them with valuable information about another slave. They always make a big show out of it as you might imagine. Basically, everyone's a potential spy. We never know who they are until the larrens let them go. Well, I know that's a bit depressing, but you were going to hear about it sooner or later and I thought you should know up front. If you have a secret, you best remember what I just said. We're all nice to each other, most of us anyway, but it's really hard to build up trust in here. And you're new. New people are always desperate to get out. So it isn't that people don't like you, but I think you'll find that most will keep their distance - at least for the first year or two. Especially the natives."

"Natives?"

"Oh, it's just what we call people who were born here - which is almost all of us. I'm a fifth generation Shift 3! We don't necessarily like it in here, but it's not so bad. This is normal for us and we don't want the fresh faces getting us in trouble. I'm sorry! That sounded meaner than I intended; not how I wanted to end our first meeting." Jenik paused, trying to think of a way to recover from the unintended rudeness, then giving up with a shrug. "Anyway, I'm sure I'll be seeing you around so let me know if you need anything."

Jenik gave Cindl a nod and Kraster a friendly punch on the shoulder then left them alone in their shack. It was tiny; one room with two sets of roughly made bunks and two sets of curtains that could be drawn to separate the room into three sections. Someone had made a cursory attempt to clean it before they got there, but it was in desperate need of some fresh air. Still, it felt good to have a little corner of the world to hide and rest.

Cindl was making a careful inspection of their new home, but Kraster sat down on the lower bunk next to the door. He watched Cindl for a few minutes trying to imagine how this must all look to her. This was her new shack as Jenik called it. After having her house in the canyon, and then the cabin at the end of the long meadow outside Lin, this was terrible. Just horrible.

"I hate larrens."

"Try not to hate them." She gave him a glance that always reminded him of his Mom.

"I can't help it. And I can't believe you can help it either."

"These larrens are cruel, but I remember the larrens on the mesa when I was a little girl. There were a couple grumpy ones, but most seemed decent. I have to believe they'd be outraged if they knew this was happening down here."

"Are you sure they don't know?"

"No, I suppose I'm not sure; but I really don't think so."

"Well I had a mesa larren lie to me and trick me into abandoning my family and now every larren I meet is either planning to kill me or work me to death as a slave."

"I don't think all the larrens down here are okay with this either."

"What! Name one nice thing they've done for us."

"There were two times in the city when I caught larrens looking at us and I would swear they were heartbroken - like they felt sorry for us."

"Well that's helpful! 'Thanks for feeling sorry for us, larrens'. Why didn't they say anything? Why didn't they attack the guards and try to free us?"

"Maybe they're in a small minority, or at least think they are. They probably just don't know what they can do. Going against the established order of things is harder than you want to admit right now."

"How can you be so calm! It just makes me so mad. I loved playing with larrens when I was a little kid. How can such great young larrens grow up to be so horrible?"

"I don't know. Humans can be that way too though."

"Not like this. Have you ever seen a human treat a larren like we've been treated? And look at us! They're going to try to work us to death in this tunnel. Well, I'm going to break out of here."

Cindl's smile forced something normal into his new abnormal world. "You probably will, knowing you. Try to relax. We'll both try to break out of here, but that'll be a lot easier if they aren't watching us all the time. Don't do anything to get their attention until you're sure you want their attention. Besides, remember how Jenik said that newbies are always the most desperate to get out? He was talking about the spying issue, but I think the bigger point is that everyone in here knows we want to escape - the other humans, and you can bet the larren guards too. So they'll be watching us more closely than normal for a while."

"But Jenik also said they won't trust us for a year or two! I don't think I can wait that long."

"Then he was right! We're desperate to get out of here, and everyone knows it. I don't want to wait two years either."

"I'm not going to spy on anyone though. I couldn't do that."

"I agree. Let's do what every other newbie probably does - bide our time and watch for a chance to escape."

"And hope we're smarter or luckier than most of them."

CHAPTER TWELVE
HANDPRINT

KRASTER SAT NERVOUSLY facing Blunt. It was obviously a nickname, but it was one of those nicknames that had become so well-worn and familiar that it completely replaced the original. He was the oldest person on the Second Shift digging crew which meant he spent a lot of time fetching tools for the younger diggers, or in this case, explaining the Creeper job to Kraster. Blunt had led Kraster about a hundred meters down the tunnel so he would be able to hear the lesson.

"I don't mean to scare you too much, but we lose a lot of creepers. You got the worst job there is."

"Really? No one told me."

"Well, you seem like a nice kid. The way I see it, you should know what you're up against. So I'm gonna tell you the risks, at least the ones we can figure out or guess at. One, you can get lost in there. These cave systems are mazes and if your globelights go out, you'll be trying to grope your way back in the blackest black you can imagine. Put it this way, I've only heard of one time when a creeper came out on his own after all his globelights had gone out. Second, you can get injured. This one isn't as bad because a lot of creepers make it out injured. Third, you get stuck. Creepers are always scared of cave ins, but you can ignore that one; I've never heard of it happening to a creeper. It happens in the main tunnel a fair amount, but I figure the caves you'll be exploring have been there a long time and if they were going to cave in, it probably would've happened a long time ago. On the other hand, if you try to go through a narrow passageway on your own in there, there isn't anyone to help you get out if you don't fit."

"Which of those is most likely to happen?"

"It's hard to know because sometime the guards won't let us send in a second creeper on a rescue mission, and we only find the missing creeper about half the time that we do go in. Usually they're dead when we find them, but we have found creepers alive that are stuck, lost or injured. Lost without a light is by far the most common though, which is why I'll be giving you an earful if you come back later than planned.

"Well, you scared me. Nice job."

"Good. You need to be careful in there. That's what I'm hoping to get pounded into your head. No heroics. Some creepers do it for decades, so don't think it's hopeless. Okay, you have all your gear? Let me see your bag."

"I think I have everything; everything they told me to bring anyway."

Blunt fingered through Kraster's bag carefully. "Looks good to me too. Okay, so remember, your goal is to see if the cave is worth following with our main tunnel. If you can find a nice big long cavern that is heading upward then it can save us a lot of digging. Got it?"

"I think so, yes."

"Your globelights should last for two days if you don't

shake them too much, but don't push it. One of the most common ways to die in there is for your globelights to go out."

"Yeah, you already mentioned that."

"Well, it's important. Maybe just go for a few hours this time."

They stood and Kraster followed Blunt back toward the head of the tunnel. The main tunnel didn't scare him at all, probably because it was full of humans and larrens. But climbing into a small black hole scared him; especially after Blunt's little chat. He had assumed he would get some practice or maybe go with another creeper a few times first to learn the job, but as they walked up the tunnel Kraster felt his stomach tighten as he realized Blunt was about to send him in alone now. Blunt was whistling an unrecognizable tune and Kraster wondered how many other creepers he had sent in for the first time. Something in that thought was like a good handhold on the cliffs, something his own courage could hang from. Others had done this before him. They were probably scared too, but they did it. He would too.

"Okay, here we are. You ready?"

"No, but go ahead and boost me up."

"There you go. You got it?"

"Yep. Thanks."

"Be careful."

Kraster climbed through the opening in the upper right part of the tunnel about ten meters back from where the rest of his shift was digging. It had been uncovered a week ago but none of the creepers on prior shifts were small enough to fit. It was tight, even for him, and he got stuck almost as soon as his feet disappeared into the cave. He was crawling on his elbows and as the cave closed in he tried to move his arms in front of him, but he couldn't. Instinctively, he tried to force it and his muscles strained against the rock. He tried harder and then even harder. The passage in front of him was completely dark and terror leapt into his mind. It was hard to breath but he desperately struggled against the immovable stone. Finally, his conscious mind broke through the panic and he forced himself to stop moving. One slow breath. A second breath. His mind cleared but he lay perfectly still to let his heart rate slow. He couldn't force the rock - that was lesson number one.

He had never experienced anything quite like it. The closest he could remember was getting his arms stuck in his shirt as a kid while trying to pull it off. He remembered trying to move his arms and the fabric stretching under the strain. The difference was that the rock of the tunnel didn't stretch.

The panic had surprised him and now embarrassed him. He never panicked on the cliffs. At least no one saw him. He had conquered his fears on the cliffs and he would do the same here. There wasn't enough room to move his arm past his head where he was now. He needed to back up until he had some room.

"Everything okay up there? I can see your feet again."

"Yeah, I'm okay. I just need to back up a bit to get my arms in front of me."

"Don't get stuck!"

"You mentioned that."

Very carefully, Kraster slid through the passageway until it opened into a larger cave. He shook his globelight and could see that it curved down and to the right. Not the way they needed it to go, but it felt great to be away from the larren guards and he decided to follow it anyway. It was very slow at first, with sharp rocks littering the bottom of the passageway.

He was amazed at the variety of surfaces as he sometimes climbed, sometimes walked, sometimes crawled further away from the main tunnel. For the first half hour he could hear the workers behind him. Gradually, he heard them less often; only when one of them yelled. Then he could only hear the picks pounding on the rock, and eventually even that faded away. He was completely alone, in the middle of a mountain, in a tiny ribbon of air surrounded by rock in every direction.

He woke to a sound. How had he fallen asleep? He couldn't remember. Had he really heard a sound or had he been dreaming? His globelight had faded but he waited to shake it. He held his breath and listened. Yes! There it was again. It was a low pitch whistle. It reminded him of the sound the wind sometimes made in a chimney. Maybe there was an opening to the outside. He gently shook his globelight and started moving as fast as he could through the cave. After another hour of crawling he was sure he could hear wind, and soon the cave opened into a chamber with giant columns of smooth, rippled, wet stone rising from floor to ceiling. At the far end, he could see starlight cutting through an opening to the outside air. Quickly, he moved across the chamber, climbed a short wall up to the lip of the opening and stepped out onto a ledge high up on the cliffs. The wind he had heard from inside now swirled and gusted around him and he closed his eyes and stretched out his arms. It was as if temporarily depriving himself of the sight somehow made it richer and his back and shoulders trembled with excitement. He couldn't keep his eyes closed for long. The horizon was just beginning to turn a lighter shade of midnight blue so he sat down and watched until it turned a brilliant orange and the sun launched into the sky illuminating everything below it.

He was able to climb up another fifteen meters above

the cave entrance, but then, like always, the handholds faded out and he had to climb back down. There was an easy route heading down from the cave entrance and it felt so good to be climbing. But it didn't go very far. The route was interrupted by a deep gouge in the rock that looked like a giant knife blade had sliced down along the cliff face. He scanned the other side for a place to land, but just before jumping, he pulled back. Something was wrong. The gouge in the rock was not perfectly vertical and he realized it was playing tricks on his eyes. He threw a few rocks across until he was sure that the landing spot on the other side was a bit higher than his current position. If he had tried to jump, he would have missed it. He looked down and froze. About twenty meters below he could make out bones spread out on the rocks where the gash closed. It was a tricky route, but he descended to the boulders. It wasn't just a few bones after all. There were dozens of skeletons. Like the girl on the cliffs, they were all small. He examined one of the skeletons closest to him and there was a small metal plate lying among the bones. It had a small hole punched on one end and he knew even before he turned it over that there would be writing on the other side.

"What is going on here!" His voice reverberated off the rocks and he felt a chill of fear creep up his neck.

There was no way to climb up the other side so Kraster reluctantly returned the way he had come and made his way to the cave entrance. Finding the girl's bones had been mystifying, but now he knew many others had made similar climbs. King Marik had clearly known why and was pleased that the humans didn't. Try as he might to think of other explanations, he was becoming convinced that the copper plates must have been a larren message being sent up the cliffs with human kids.

But what message could be so important that they would send dozens, probably hundreds of kids to their death? He didn't understand what was going on, but something bad had happened. He knew that much.

Back inside the cavern, he noticed signs that others had been there. There were scratch marks on the stone columns that looked like attempts to keep track of time, and a few names carefully etched as a permanent record. There were piles of stacked stones; one almost as tall as himself. Then he found the wall. It was a smooth dry wall, covered with hundreds of brown hand prints, all of them were smaller than his own. It only took a moment to instinctively understand. These were the signatures of kids who knew they were lost. Over a hundred kids, each adding their mark, finding a measure of peace in knowing that they were part of a larger group.

Kraster hesitated for a moment. He wasn't part of the same horror that they endured, but he knew his handprint belonged with theirs. He was being sent to his death by larrens too. Kraster had to try three times before he scraped his hand hard enough to draw blood, but then he coaxed enough out to coat his own hand, found a spot on the wall and added his hand print.

His thoughts were a jumble. Why should he go back and dig for the larrens? The larren king knew what had happened on these cliffs. That much had been clear during their interrogation. He would rather die than help the larrens dig a tunnel up to where his sister and parents lived. If he was going to die anyway, he would rather do it peacefully here in the cave than working for the larrens, but he had to try to protect Cindl, and he had to find a way to fight the larrens.

CHAPTER THIRTEEN
BEST DAY

Myree was transformed by her new freedom. Although, getting back to the secret houses had been harder than she would have guessed. First, she had to get stronger so she could handle both the pull-ups onto the roof and the climb back up through the crack in the cliff. She was dying to show someone, but she couldn't think of an alternative reason why she would be doing all these pull-ups and in the end she had to keep her new strength a secret too.

The bigger difficulty was figuring out how to schedule long blocks of time. Pretending to be sick would only work a few times. Instead, she developed a second group of friends so both groups would think she was with the other on the weekends. The biggest surprise was how happy she'd become. She laughed more often and even got in trouble for talking too much in class. That had never happened before and she felt a mix of embarrassment and pride. Fortunately, she was turning fourteen next week and everyone seemed to expect big changes like this.

It took three months to line up a whole afternoon when

she wouldn't be missed, and now she crouched behind a tree only ten meters from the edge of the main cliffs. It was a sunny and cold Saturday afternoon in December, but there wasn't much wind and she was comfortable in her coat. The climb down out of town had been easy, but it took over an hour to carefully move through the surrounding farms without being seen. The caution was worth it. It had been more than five years and she could feel the emotion rising in her throat. She couldn't wait and listen forever, so she stood and stepped out into the open. There was nothing but grass between her and the edge and she started crying as she walked closer. It was the best kind of crying; the kind that comes in waves, but leaves you feeling lighter and stronger when it's all over. She peeked over the edge. It was just like she remembered. Even better; the natural beauty mixed with the sweetness of nostalgia. The smallness of the mesa impressed her as it never had when she was younger. As big as it was, and as large and rugged as the base might be, it was all just a small mound in the much larger desert. The horizon was hazy as the wind kicked up the cold dry sand, but she remembered how far away it looked on clear days.

She needed to sit and think. There was a boulder to her left and she made herself comfortable. It was good to be alone. As much as she thought of her brother before, being here, looking down at the base made him more real again. He had been fading without her realizing it. But in the space of a few minutes he had come alive again in her mind. She always talked about him in the past tense so the adults wouldn't worry about her. Now she wondered if talking about him that way had slowly killed him in her own mind. Being here changed everything. Those ridges below might hide his new home. Maybe his grave. But like in the past, she couldn't just accept that he was dead. The wind picked up and she pulled her coat tighter around her neck.

She heard a gasp behind her and jumped to her feet. A young larren had stopped a few meters away with her eyes fixed on Myree and a look of surprise and confusion on her face. She was beautiful. Her short thick fur was a smooth dark brown, almost black, but she had a wide golden brown stripe running down her back. She had been walking on all fours, but now she stood up.

"What are you doing here?"

"Nothing. What are you doing here?"

The larren paused and then smiled. "I'm sorry. That was a horrible start! You surprised me I guess. I'm not sure I'm allowed to be over here, so I'm a little jumpy."

"Me too obviously! Sorry. I'm not really supposed to be here either."

"You've been crying? Are you okay?"

Myree had been hoping it wasn't obvious, but now she wiped her eyes. "Yeah. I haven't been to the edge in five years and… I guess all the memories… It's hard to explain."

"Don't be embarrassed. Five years. Wow. That's a long time. Did you just turn sixteen?"

"No, I'll be fourteen in seven days. I found a way to sneak out of town about three months ago, but today's the first day I made it to the cliffs. Do I really look sixteen?"

"I don't know. I never see human kids anymore. It's sad isn't it?"

"Very sad. Wait, larrens aren't allowed on this side of the river anymore?"

"I'm not sure. There's no official rule, but everyone stays

on their sides now. Besides, if they find a young larren like me wandering around on the human side, everyone would be nervous I was looking for a kid to make the jump with. Wilton and Kraster really ruined things didn't they?"

Myree couldn't help but smile. Back in town, at least around her, no one would have said anything suggesting Kraster was at fault. It was refreshing to hear someone talk about it so honestly.

"Kraster was my brother." She waited for her words to sink in. "You're expression is hilarious! Don't worry, you didn't offend me. You can't tell anyone you met me out here okay? I can't believe I even told you."

"You're Myree?"

"That's me. And seriously, if anyone finds out I'm outside of town, they'll start watching me while I sleep and I'll never get out again."

"I won't say anything. But what are the chances! You were with them when they made the jump?"

"Yep. It seems so long ago sometimes."

"It really does. So, what was Wilton like? The elders all make him out to be this terrible criminal."

"Well, keep in mind I was only eight at the time, but he seemed really normal. I liked him. Kraster really liked him, but that might just have been because he was quite a bit older than we were. For a few years afterward I really hated him, and I still do a little, but after feeling trapped in town for so long, I have a little sympathy for him. Not much. Just a little."

Ena studied Myree carefully, trying to decide how much she could trust her. "I've always wondered if he wasn't really so bad. If I said that out loud back home, I'd be in so much trouble."

"Same here. Hey, I don't know your name."

"I'm Ena."

"I'm really glad you found me, Ena. It's been hard having this secret with no one to tell. How old are you, by the way?"

"I'm fourteen. I'm only two months older than you. My birthday was in October."

"So, hold on, you said most larrens don't cross the river. How often do you come over here?"

"Maybe once a week. No, probably every other week. I try to come about once a week, but sometimes there are too many larrens or humans around and I have to give up. But once I get over here, it's so quiet and peaceful. You're the only person I've ever come across on this stretch of the edge."

"I wonder why? I love it here. I'm definitely coming back."

"When will you be back? I'll try to meet you again."

"I can't next weekend."

"Oh yeah, your birthday party right?"

"Yeah. How about the next Saturday after that?"

"I can't promise, but I'll try hard to be here."

The rest of the afternoon passed quickly but finally Myree knew she had to head back. It would be stupid to push her luck. Still, it had been one of the best days of her life and she hated to cut it off. The excitement of climbing down and out of town, seeing the cliffs and base again, and unexpectedly, finding a new friend.

Climbing back up was easier than she expected. Next time she wouldn't bring a rope.

CHAPTER FOURTEEN

DEEP DOWN

A YEAR IN THE tunnel had turned Kraster into a young man. He was sixteen and like all sixteen-year-old boys, he couldn't help marveling at his own muscles. He sometimes wondered what he would be like as a sixteen-year-old on the mesa. One thing was certain, he wouldn't be this strong or fast. The training for the Rain Games hadn't hurt either. For the last two months the whole camp was focused on the upcoming Games, and more specifically on the Wall and Hammer tournament. Last year, he had watched the tournament with a mixture of shock and fascination. It was by far the roughest game he'd ever seen.

Each match was held in the circle courtyard in the middle of camp, with the spectators crowded in on two sides so that the circle was transformed into a rectangular playing field that was roped off for the games. All the houses that ringed the courtyard were built with large windows on their second floor that looked out over the crowd. These were the best seats for the matches and you had to be invited. The kids fought for spots on the roofs and by the time a match started, every conceivable spot was occupied. Everyone was yelling and laughing and eating. It was happy and rough and the atmosphere crackled with excitement. The first match of the tournament was always Shift One against Shift Two, and it was held two days after Shift Two got back from the tunnel. Then Shift Two would play Shift Three two days after they got back from the tunnel and so on until Shift Four played Shift One. Every year the larrens set aside one week in the spring and one in the fall when the humans were not required to work on the tunnel, and the week in October was when the final Wall and Hammer match took place. The first four matches were held leading up to that week. The scores from those first round of matches were used to determine which shifts competed in the final.

The game was simple. Each shift fielded forty players and each shift had their color. Shift One was red, Shift Two was green, Shift Three was yellow, and Shift Four was blue. One player on each team was designated as "The Larren". They had to wear a white shirt and paint their face in their team's color. Twenty players were collectively called the Wall. They wore black shirts and also painted their faces. Their only job was to prevent the other team from getting to their larren. The remaining 19 players were called the Hammer. Each member of the Hammer wore a shirt in their team's color and would dip their hands in paint of the same color. Their main job was to get that paint on the opposing Larren's white shirt. As soon as that was accomplished, the game was over. If you won in the first five minutes - round one- your shift got five points. If you won in the next five minutes - round two - you got four points, and so on down to one point for a win that occurred after the 20th minute. There was no time limit however, and on rare occasions round five would drag on for several hours.

Each shift had to field at least five players who were seventeen or younger. One of these five was always designated as the larren, but that left four spots for active players. The Wall was almost always composed of the biggest and strongest players, so the four youngest players were traditionally always in the Hammer. These four were called the Runts and being selected as a Runt was about the greatest thing that could happen to a boy.

Last year, Kraster had watched the matches from the rooftops with his best friend Bend. This year they had both been picked for the Second Shift Green Runts. Almost everyone else on the team was in their late twenties or thirties, and they loved teasing the Runts about how small and fragile they were. But every boy dreamed of being one of the Runts. Kraster and Bend could hardly believe it when they found out. Usually, the Runts from each shift would face off during the match - it was like a miniature match inside the bigger match. Bend and Kraster had trained incredibly hard. Fortunately, there hadn't been any caves to explore recently, so Kraster had been able to dig with the rest of his shift which was a much better workout than climbing through caves.

The first match against the Shift One Reds had almost been a disaster. Red's Hammer came close to breaking through Green's Wall in minute three which would have given Shift One the full five points. But Green rallied and ended up winning for two points in the 18th minute. The second game, against the Third Shift Yellows, had been the key win. Usually there was a big surge of activity at the end of each point window as both teams tried to win the game before the point level dropped. Then there was a lull a the beginning of the new point window as each team tried to catch their breath. After the bell rang ending the five-point window, Green's hammer had turned and started trotting back toward their side like normal, but they were each counting to seven in their heads. On seven, they all turned around and rushed the Yellow Wall in one spot. It had worked perfectly. Yellow's Wall was caught off their guard just enough for the Green Hammer to break through, and in a frantic fight Shift One tagged Shift Three's Larren to end the game for four points. Those four points were enough to put Green in the final match against Blue.

The Wall and Hammer tournament had been going on for 218 years -this was the 219th tournament - and Blue had the most wins. In fact, they had won the tournament for the last four years straight and had won eleven of the twenty tournaments before that. Bend had taken Kraster to see the Rain Games tally in the Mayor's house shortly after he arrived. The last time the Shift Two Greens had won the tournament was fifteen years ago.

"Kraster! Over here!" Bend was surrounded by about a dozen younger boys and girls and had obviously been dazzling them with details about being a Green Runt. "So, Kraster here was even closer than I was in that last rush against Yellow. What do you think of that?"

The kids stared at Kraster as if he were a giant, then started asking him questions and telling him how amazing he was.

"All right, all right. Off you go! Kraster and I have to do some training for the final." The kids reluctantly wandered off. "So, what kind of training should we do?"

Kraster laughed and shoved Bend against a nearby shack. "Well, we should at least go somewhere else so those kids don't realize you're a liar. You nervous?"

"Are you kidding? I've never felt so nervous! I know we're

supposed to rest today but I'm so jittery I might as well be working out."

"I'm not that nervous. Weird isn't it? I think I'll be nervous tomorrow."

"I wish I was you!"

Although being picked for the team had been a shock to Kraster, he assumed Bend would be picked. Bend was a month younger but he was bigger and stronger than Kraster. The first time they met was after Kraster's second time in the tunnel. Kids born in the camp didn't start working until they were 15, but slaves brought in from outside were always thrown in right away. Bend had found this very insulting as it was obvious he was stronger than Kraster. Like so many things, he was eager to start doing what the adults would have loved to stop doing. Kraster wasn't used to being insulted and their shouting match devolved into a full blown fight. When the adults pulled them apart two minutes later, they were both bloody but neither was beaten. In the strange world of boyhood, they had been best friends ever since.

"Hey, let's grab supper and go eat it on Mek's roof."

"Yeah, okay."

Ten minutes later they were sitting on a roof at the edge of camp. The house was right next to the first wall and Kraster loved to sit there looking out at the forests beyond. He had found the spot about six months ago. It reminded him of the route he'd found back near Lin because no one else seemed to know about it. You had to jump from one roof, to a second roof, and finally to Mek's roof. The jumps weren't particularly difficult, but the camp slaves just didn't have the same climber's instincts. Bend had been hesitant to try it when Kraster first showed him the way, but now this was their sanctuary; this was where the deep conversations happened.

They ate silently for several minutes, enjoying the colors seeping into the evening sky. Bend could only stay quiet for short stretches.

"You know, I can't help think that someday I'm going to come looking for you and I'll find out you escaped. You won't tell me ahead of time because you know I'd be nervous to leave."

"Would you be mad at me?"

"Well, yeah I'd be mad!"

"I'd love to escape, but I can't see how."

"Well you could jump the first wall easy from this roof, or from a hundred other roofs for that matter."

"And then the larrens would spot me while I tried to climb the next two. I still have a hard time accepting that you don't want to leave."

"Kraster, for the millionth time, it isn't that I don't want to leave, I just wouldn't know where to go. You're the one that told us the free humans have no idea about any of this. I doubt I could even get there. At least here I've got my family and friends. At least here I'm a Green Runt!"

"Shhhh! Keep it down!"

"Look, I get it, your family's up there. Everyone loves you here but you're an outsider. You don't completely fit in."

"What do you mean?! Of course I fit in."

"No. Not really. I was thinking about it last week and the best way I can say it is that you're not a slave. I mean, obviously you are a slave, but it's like you don't know you're a slave. Deep down, you're not a slave. I think almost all the rest of us are."

"I don't believe that. Look at Wall and Hammer. The

reason the game was invented in the first place was so that we would be fighters. Remember? We're all strong from working the tunnel, but that's different than being a fighter. The whole point was to make sure that we were also an army ready to fight when the time came."

"Yeah, but Kraster, that was 218 years ago! That proves my point. We say we want to fight, or at least be ready to fight, but here we are sitting on Mek's roof two hundred years later and we've never actually fought. We go through the motions, but I don't think most of us really believe we can ever be free."

"Nope. I don't buy it. I think there's still a fire burning deep down."

CHAPTER FIFTEEN

RAIN GAMES

THE BELL RANG and the first round started. Kraster, Bend and the other two Green Runts led the first surge. Behind them the rest of the Green Hammer rushed after them. The first surge was traditional, almost ceremonial. Those in front tried to bowl over as many as possible so that the progressively bigger players behind them could keep charging toward the opposing wall. Almost nothing was ever accomplished in this first surge, but it was a test of strength that let everyone see whose Hammer was stronger. Kraster was at the very front as the smallest player in the Hammer and rushed toward his counterpart in Blue's Hammer. As Kraster and Bend had practiced, at the last moment Kraster veered to his left and slammed his right forearm against his opponent's head sending him spinning down into a heap. Then he dove at the second Blue and both fell to the ground swinging and kicking. Perfect! He had taken down two blues. The boy he was fighting finally got his arm free and punched Kraster hard in the face, but it didn't matter, the first surge was already over. Despite Kraster's good start, Blue was a bigger team and they had rebounded well. It wasn't a dominating performance, but Blue looked like the stronger Hammer.

The game downshifted to a more methodical pace with each side running around trying to coalesce into a formation that looked like a mismatch in their favor, then they would surge forward against the Wall. It was exhausting. The Blue Runts seemed to have one strategy: knocking the Green Runts out of the game. They ignored the Green Wall and just attacked the Green Runts relentlessly. This was a new twist. Two of them had just ganged up on Bend and had been pounding on him until Kraster finally arrived to even it up.

"We need a plan! Oh wow Bend. Can you see out of your eye?"

"Yeah. Well, a little. He got me good. So what's the plan?"

"I'm still working on one, but I know it has to take advantage of the fact that they only seem to have one plan."

"What if their plan is to just attack us for a certain amount of time - long enough for us to get used to it - and then change their strategy and attack the Wall?"

"You're right. That would be a good strategy. We'll have to watch for that."

The bell rang for the second round. The points didn't really matter in the final match, but everyone still liked to keep track of how long it had taken to win. The Green Runts made several attempts to get through the Blue Wall, but the Blue Runts were always right on their tail and they never even made a dent. Meanwhile the Green Wall was holding, but barely. The Blue Hammer was powerful and they had trained hard, so it was a bit surprising when the bell sounded for the third round and they still hadn't lost. Finally, a plan started to form in Kraster's mind. It would take advantage of the fact that the Blue Runts continued to hound them and the way the Blue Wall defended.

The Blue Wall had perfected a defense called "the inside float". Their Wall used twelve members to form the outer ring. They would hold each other's arms and maintained an even distance between them, only letting go of each other when the opposing Hammer struck. Inside that outer ring, was the inside float. The remaining eight members of the Wall would surge to whatever side was being attacked. They were usually smaller than those on the outside ring, but they were fast and could move to reinforce whoever needed it in a flash. Other shifts had tried to copy them over the years, but no one did it better than Blue.

Kraster explained his plan to the other Runts one at a time as they ran around the field. He thought about trying to let the rest of the Hammer know, but decided it would be best if only the Runts knew. They drifted over to the right side of the field about half way between the two Walls, staying close enough together so that they would be able to hear Kraster's signal. They kept moving and entering little skirmishes with the Blue Runts just to make sure they didn't sense something was going on.

The crowd on south side of the field started cheering wildly, which didn't make any sense. The game momentarily stopped as everyone looked at the crowd trying to understand what they were cheering about. A raindrop landed on Kraster's nose at the same moment that he noticed the crowd was looking up at the sky. It was raining! In another few seconds everyone understood as the rain swept across the field to the crowd on the opposite side. Even the players joined in the cheering now. It had rained for a week during the first Wall and Hammer tournament, but rain in October was unusual. And then the thunder rolled through the clouds overhead. Kraster had never heard cheering so loud. He could feel the goose bumps forming on his arms but it was impossible to tell if they were from the rain's chill or the excitement in the air.

The rain started falling harder and when the game resumed every player was smiling. Even with all the details of the game rushing through his mind, Kraster understood that this was a historic match. People would be talking about it for a long time and he was in it! One of the Blue runts surprised Kraster from the side and forced him fully back into the game. Something about the rain, about the significance of this match, made him want to win even more than he had before. They still had their plan and he thought it should still work in the rain.

Finally, the rest of the Green Hammer formed up and surged at the Blue Wall over on the left side. The inside float instantly congealed against them on the left side leaving only the outside ring to defend the right side. Kraster gave the signal as soon as he saw the surge begin and the other three Green Runts rushed toward the Blue Wall's right side from wherever they were. Kraster hung back a few seconds then sprinted after them. They had picked a specific man on the right side who was the tallest in that section. With the Blue Runts in pursuit, Bend slammed into the tall defender who managed to stop him without too much trouble. Then the second Green Runt dove at his legs before the Blue Runts piled on top of them. The third Green Runt threw himself on top of the Blue Runts just in time for Kraster to use the whole pile as a springboard to jump up and over the wall. The tall defender's feet had been hit and he was off balance and bent over to fight off the Runts. Kraster soared over the battle, and in a split second, he was inside the Blue Wall. The Blue Larren saw what was happening and screamed for help just in time for one of the inside floaters and another defender from the outside ring to jump to his defense. Kraster swung his fist as hard as he could at one of the defenders, but the other met him in the air and pulled him to the ground away from the Blue Larren. They fought frantically and Kraster tried desperately to reach out and touch the white shirt. He could feel himself being punched and kicked but he was clawing closer and the Blue Larren was backing away toward the outer ring. All around him, the Blue Wall was falling apart as the normal order gave way to full blown chaos now that a Green was inside the wall. The pile on top of him kept getting heavier and he couldn't see anything anymore, but then he heard the gong start ringing over and over. The game was over and even from the bottom of the pile he could hear the crowd. Someone's stomach was still pressing the side of his face firmly into the muddy grass, but he caught the first hint of his name. "Kraster! Kraster! Kraster!" It got louder and louder as the chant spread through the crowd. The pile of fighters pulled themselves off one or two at a time until finally Kraster was pulled up out of the mud by the captain of the Blue Wall. As soon as the crowd saw Kraster emerge from the bottom of the pile, the cheering surged in volume.

"But I didn't make it to your Larren."

"No, but your little stunt cracked the wall. You're something else kid. Congratulations."

Kraster was too embarrassed to say anything, but he didn't have time anyway. The rest of the Shift Two Green's hoisted him up on their shoulders and paraded through the rain, and Kraster smiled until it hurt to smile.

CHAPTER SIXTEEN
ANOTHER WORLD

Myree was led through a massive hallway by the oldest larren she had ever seen. The walls were covered with incredible paintings - murals really. Some of the scenes stretched along the wall for at least ten meters but she couldn't stop and take them in. She wished Ena was with her, but her guide insisted that Ena wait outside. The whole thing was strange. She and Ena had been meeting by the cliffs for several months but someone must have finally seen them. And now Jesh himself wanted to talk to her. His representatives told Ena to bring Myree to see him at their next meeting and so here she was. She had heard of Jesh - everyone had - but she'd never met him. He had tried to come visit her shortly after Kraster jumped but her parents wouldn't allow it. When she heard people talk about him, it was clear he was respected even by most of the humans.

The hallway opened into a large, sunny, circular room. On the opposite side, a large archway opened out to thin air and she could see the desert horizon. This room must sit right at the edge of the cliff. The next thing she noticed was the garden instead of a typical floor. It was probably beautiful in the spring and summer, but in January most of the plants were dormant. Even without the extra colors, the room was extraordinary. The walls and columns were covered with carved flowers, trees and dozens of intricate patterns. Evergreen vines climbed the walls in various places and Myree wondered who would let such beautiful art become overgrown with vines. Finally, the ceiling was a very large dome painted a deep blood-red. The dome rested on a ring of smaller archways to let in sunlight.

"Jesh will see you now." The old larren gave what must have been a smile, then turned and walked back down the hallway leaving Myree alone at the top of the pathway leading down into the garden.

"Thank you for coming Myree. I should tell you, this is the first time we've ever let a human into the Crimson Room."

"It's beautiful! Is it a temple?"

"Hmm, I suppose you could think of it as a temple, though I've never really thought of it that way. I'm afraid I cannot tell you the whole story behind this room, but when I heard the human girl exploring the cliffs was Kraster's sister, I decided to break our rule. I have to ask, are you considering a jump yourself?"

"Well, no, I'm just trying to find a way to climb down the cliffs, I wouldn't…" Myree stopped. That was the answer she knew she should offer, but there was a struggle beneath it. "Maybe. I don't know yet. I've thought about it. I know I shouldn't."

"I agree, you shouldn't. You've put me in a difficult position."

"I'm sorry."

"No, don't be, let me finish. What I should do is to inform

my human counterpart that a girl has found a way outside the walls and is mingling with a young larren. But as you know, I have been vehemently opposed to those walls from the beginning and I'm thrilled that someone found a way out. If you were anyone else, I would not have interfered at all, but your family already lost Kraster. So I've decided to take the rather controversial step of bringing a human into one of our most secret places. This will surprise you, but only about forty larrens even know that this place exists. But that's unimportant. Although I don't think you should make the jump, I realize that you might chose to do so in search of your brother. In the event that you disregard my advice and the advice that you can imagine your parents would give you, I at least want to give you the best chance of returning that I am able to give. If you stay on the mesa, may I ask you to keep the information I'm about to share a secret?"

"For how long?"

Jesh looked pleased with the question. "For the rest of your life unless I give you permission to share it. I'm offering you valuable information, but if you stay, a secret can be a heavy burden."

Myree looked around the room to give herself a moment to think. She had been talking to Ena about jumping. They hadn't made a final decision, but she knew she wanted to. Maybe not today or this month, but she knew she would want to in the future.

"Okay, I agree to keep your secret."

"Turn around. Look back above the door you came through."

"What is it? Is that a map?"

"It is a legendary route up the cliffs."

"Really!"

"Please don't make the jump based on the assumption that you can climb back up. As you can see, this is a very old map and there is no one alive who can confirm that it's real. That said, I'm nervous you might jump, and this is one thing I can do that might allow you to return to your family."

"How come I've never heard of this before. If you would show this to the rest of the humans, the walls would come down and you'd have a thousand humans lining up to make the jump. I don't understand why this is a secret."

"No, and as I said when you first came in, there are some things that I cannot tell you that would answer your question. Believe me, we've been arguing over that very idea as long as I've been on the Larren Council; long before the walls went up. But I won't trouble you with our council debates. What matters now is that I've decided to show it to you. This is a small way for me - for all of us larrens - to apologize for what happened to your brother."

"Do we know where it starts? Down below I mean. If I were down there, where would I find the beginning?"

"If the legends are true, then it should start almost directly below this place. As you can see on the map, there is a natural archway that marks the beginning. I would ask you to study the map as long as you need to, but then to keep it a secret until the Larren Council decides to make it known. And one last thing. This pendant was made by your human ancestors a very long time ago. It won't mean anything to a human, but bring this to the larren king. I think he will know it came from me and you will have his protection."

"It's beautiful. I've never seen anything like it! Humans made this?"

"Yes; a long time ago. I think you've lost this craft over the centuries, but as you can see, humans have the capacity for remarkable things! There is another very old story that the stone in that pendant came from another world."

"Is that true?"

"I don't know. It's always so hard to sort the real from the unreal in very old stories, but sometimes the story itself is wonderful and worth keeping, don't you think? I remember when I first heard that story. I could hardly wait until it got dark so I could go out and look at the stars. With that little story in my mind, it was like looking at the sky for the first time. Now, I can't look at the expanse of stars without wondering if I'm staring at another world. Regardless, it's incredibly rare. We've never found another stone like it."

"You're giving it to me?"

"I've always thought it should be in the hands of a human anyway. Why not you?"

"But how will larrens down below know this came from you? Is that something else you can't tell me?"

"I'm afraid I can't tell you the full answer. However, what I choose to tell you is that I believe that this pendant will be legendary among the larrens below; that I think they will recognize it and know I gave it to you. And I hope it will provide some protection if you need it."

"I had no idea there were so many secrets."

"Hopefully not forever. Now, I'll stop talking and let you memorize the map. Put the pendant on so you don't lose it."

"Why do you want me to make the jump?"

Jesh moved to speak and then stopped, a genuine smile spreading across his face. "Myree, I like you so much more than I expected! You've seen through all the motion to focus on the most important question. You had me at a loss for words and that's rare. I can't answer your question directly. But regardless of what I want, I promise you the decision will remain yours."

Myree put the thin chain over her head and examined the pendant in more detail. She had only seen gold a few times before but she recognized it immediately. The chain was a weave of gold and another white metal she didn't recognize. The pendant contained a brilliant yellow stone at the center unlike anything she'd ever seen. It was as large as a human iris and, other than the yellow color, was perfectly clear. Light reflected off the smooth facets making the stone shimmer as she moved it. Surrounding the stone was an intricate design made out of wire in the same two colors as the chain. They shot out from the central stone like stylized rays of the sun in long narrow loops.

"It looks like the sun. Not like the real sun, but like an artist's picture of the sun."

"Then you won't be surprised that we call it 'The Sun Pendant', although I don't know for certain if that was the original intent."

Myree sat down and stared at the giant painting over the doorway. As Jesh said, it was old and there were places where the plaster had fallen away leaving empty patches. But the route was still clear. It wasn't really a map as much as a progression of visual markers with arrows to indicate a direction. After a big gap with an "X" on the wall, you were supposed to go left. She assumed it would make sense when you were climbing.

After about ten minutes, she rose, thanked Jesh for the pendant and the map, then left following the same old larren back to where Ena waited.

CHAPTER SEVENTEEN
LAST DAY

THE LAST CLASS of the day was over and Myree had walked out of school for the last time. Earlier that morning she had kissed her mom's cheek for the last time. Last night, she hugged her dad for the last time before she went to bed. Technically it might not be the last time, but she didn't know for sure. So it had felt like it might be her last walk to school, her last lunch with her friends. Each last was a chance to change her mind and each last time felt like it had little fingers reaching out to pull her back from the edge. Every step forward required a force of will. It reminded her of making the decision to plunge into cool water, like she did as a kid at the river. Especially if she had waded in a little first. The parts of her body that had been underwater for a while would feel fine, but every little step deeper would make her cringe as it exposed a new strip of skin to the cool water. Every step deeper required a decision. Eventually, she would work up the courage to throw herself completely underwater.

Before the last class her teacher had asked her if she was okay. She hoped she didn't look as nervous as she felt, but she was sure her teacher followed her to the door and watched her leave for home. Maybe her Mom had noticed she was acting strange and sent a message to the school. The crowd of kids dwindled as they each broke off on their own routes home. It was time to make her decision; either go straight toward home, or turn left and head for the south end of town. She had been wading in a centimeter at a time but now it was time for the plunge. In almost exactly the same way, she paused to gather her courage, to build up the determination she needed, then she turned left.

Everything was familiar now. The old building with the hole in the ceiling, the careful crawl along the roofs, the ladder down to the secret old houses, and the climb down the crack to her freedom. The only difference was the rendezvous point. The last time they met, Ena was sure she was being followed and they decided to meet somewhere new next time. Myree could tell something was wrong as soon as she saw Ena.

"What is it?"

"There are larrens all over the place; mostly along the edge. I think someone must suspect we're planning to make the jump. You didn't notice anything?"

"Well, maybe, but I'm so nervous I thought I might just be paranoid."

"You obviously made it out here so they must not have been watching you too close."

"No, I guess not. But Jesh wants us to jump. Why would larrens be out trying to stop us? It doesn't make any sense."

"I don't know either. Maybe he changed his mind, or maybe he didn't think we would jump this soon. Are you sure he wanted us to jump?"

"I asked him. He didn't admit to anything, but he could

have denied it. I'm almost positive he wants us to jump. Maybe someone else found out and he can't say anything without getting himself in trouble."

"That's possible. Look, whatever the reason, should we reconsider? I mean, we need to be really sure about this. I hate feeling like Jesh is just using us and we don't know why."

Myree didn't know how to respond. She had agonized over this decision so long and she didn't want to drag it all up again in her mind. "You can tell me if you don't want to go, Ena. I still want to do this, but I have a chance of climbing back. This is permanent for you - I get that. So I don't want you to do this just because of me. If I pressure you to do this, I'm no different than Wilton."

"No, it's not that. I want to go. Larrens don't have the same family structures, so this is a lot easier for me. But Myree, your parents love you, you've told me that yourself. Are you sure you can leave them? We don't know if Kraster's still alive and this might be permanent for you too."

All the old doubts started to resurface in Myree's mind, but she felt her resolve stiffening in response. "Thank you, Ena. I can tell you're trying to protect me from a mistake, but I know what I want to do. My parents will still have each other, but if Kraster is alive down there, then he's alone. And part of that is my fault. Don't argue with me, I know it's not all my fault. But Kraster might need help. Thanks to Jesh, I have a pendant that should get me help from the King and at least some hope of a way back home. This is how I can right something I did wrong. If you're still willing, I'd like to go find my brother."

"Okay, I just wanted to make sure. I'd still like to go."

"And... don't laugh, because I'm being really serious. It does feel like we're walking into some trap or trick, so I just want to tell you ahead of time that I promise I'll watch out for you. If I can protect you or help you, I will."

Ena smiled but didn't laugh. "I promise the same thing. We're in this together, okay?"

"Okay. So how are we going to get to the cliffs without being stopped?"

"I have an idea for that. I think you should tie yourself on my back now and then I'll carry you to the edge. Then, if we can find a gap, we can just make a run for it and jump right off. That might be easier anyway so I don't have time to freak out at the edge."

"I like it. Can you carry me that far?"

"Sure! You're light remember? That's the whole point of pairing up for the jump."

"I just hate making you carry me before you have to."

Behind them, from the human side they heard some people yelling and then they could hear that they were yelling Myree's name. This was it. Their plan was discovered. The larrens that were looking for them must be able to hear the humans too so they would be looking even harder now.

"We better go." Myree had brought the rope and they rigged it up like she has seen it done six years before. Like all larrens, the patagiums that stretched between Ena's arms and legs had been pierced close to her body when she was very young. That allowed a rope to be threaded through the piercings and tied around her torso while still allowing her to stretch out the patagiums for gliding. Not all larrens ended up needing the piercings, but they all received them just in case. Myree tied herself onto Ena's back and made sure her arms were aligned so she could help support Ena's arms on the long glide down.

"Last chance Myree. Are you sure about this?"

"I'm sure. Let's go."

Ena started moving carefully through a small gully that wound its way toward the cliffs, but it was hard going. It was full of bushes and mud which not only made it hard to navigate, they made quiet movement almost impossible. The shouts were getting louder as the humans were clearly spreading out and moving quickly.

"I think we should get out of this gully - what do you think Myree? It's too slow."

"Sure. How far do you think we are from the cliff?"

"Well, we were probably 300 meters away when we started and we've gone maybe 50 through this gully. We have to move faster."

"Okay. Do it."

They climbed out of the gully and were spotted immediately by a group of humans moving in their direction.

"Ena, run!"

There was no more sneaking. This was a frantic dash for the edge. Myree briefly tried to look around to help spot humans or larrens but all her attention shifted to surviving the ride. She was tied onto Ena's back and Ena was running on all fours. There wasn't much chance of her falling off, but her upper body and head were being slammed up and down against Ena's back and shoulders. She tried holding herself flat against Ena's back but it wouldn't work. Instead all her strength and attention when into cushioning the movement.

Ena stopped abruptly and Myree looked up. Twenty meters in front of them were two larrens blocking the gap between two groups of trees. Ena paused only for a second, then looking to either side picked right and turned into the trees. It was slower but they were temporarily out of anyone's view. The slower pace was easier on Myree so she couldn't help appreciate the change.

"Ena, turn right again. There! Quick. I have an idea."

"Myree, that's the wrong way. The cliff's to the left."

"I know. Those larrens are probably moving through the trees behind us now, trying to find us. And they're going to assume that we'll veer to the left."

"I have been veering to the left."

"So let's make a hard turn right, and then another right and double back to the path where we started."

"What if there are other larrens or humans there now?"

"I don't know. Then we'll be in trouble - like we are now."

"Okay, fine. Let's try it."

They moved through the trees as quickly as they could and looped back toward the original route. It was hard knowing they were moving away from their goal, but so far it was working. They couldn't hear anyone behind them. Ena slowed down as they approached the edge of the trees.

"Do you see anything? I don't hear anything."

"No, I don't either. I can't think of a reason to wait."

Ena burst out of the trees and ran as fast as she could. The previously guarded gap was now wide open and as they went through they could see the cliff edge up ahead for the first time. But to their left another group of larrens spotted them and ran along the cliff edge trying to cut them off. Now it was just a race to see if Ena could make it to the cliff before the larrens could stop them. Myree focused on protecting herself without slowing Ena down.

The larrens were faster without anyone to carry and they closed fast. The one in the lead reached them just as they were getting to the edge and lunged to knock them over. He rammed into Myree's left leg and Ena's side just as Ena was jumping. Instead of a graceful leap, they left the mesa spinning in a circle. Myree screamed as they plummeted downward. Ena worked to get some control and finally managed to stop the spin, and after a few moments of terror the freefall was over. They glided out away from the cliffs, but then, as they had discussed over the last few months, Ena turned and started gliding parallel to the cliff face rather than away from it.

Myree tried to look back to see if anyone was watching them, but they had already dropped too far and she couldn't even be sure where they had jumped from."

"That was the scariest thing I've ever experienced in my entire life!"

Ena just laughed. Myree could feel it more than hear it. It was hard to talk with the wind howling in their ears and it was hard to see as it stung their eyes.

"You see anything?"

"Not yet. Don't dive yet."

"I won't."

"Hey! Over there - up ahead and to the right. Is that a village?"

"I can't see it yet."

"I think it is! Veer to the right just a little. Too much. Okay - perfect! Should we try the dive idea?"

Ena answered by going into a steeper dive and they could feel their speed increase dramatically. The plan was to shave some minutes off the glide time since they were younger than most jumpers. But this was scarier than they imagined. Ena said something, but Myree couldn't hear it. She shouted back, but they were going too fast to talk. The village was very clearly in front of them now and Ena was heading straight toward it.

"Let's level out!!!" Myree screamed and tried to pull back on Ena's shoulders to signal her idea. Ena nodded and they both worked to slow their descent. There was a small street running between a row of cottages and Ena banked to their left and then back to the right to align their approach with the street. People were coming out of cottages and pointing up at them. Someone must have seen them and let everyone know.

It was working, they were slowing down, but still coming in fast.

"Okay, I need everything!"

Myree pushed down with every ounce of strength she had. It was over almost before she was ready. The wind died down and Ena dropped them gently into the middle of the road. No rolling or skidding. After a moment's silence the crowd erupted in cheers and gathered around the new arrivals.

CHAPTER EIGHTEEN

FIERCE

"WHAT'S GOING ON up there?" The questions started even before someone cut the rope holding Myree against Ena's back. She tried to answer but was interrupted by other questions before she could finish. Ena tried answering a few with the same result. After the initial rush of excitement at the landing, Myree wished she could sneak away. The crowd was getting larger and a few of the adults were increasingly agitated that their questions weren't being answered. She was glancing at one of them when she remembered she had her own question.

"Hey, is Kraster down here?" The question quieted the crowd momentarily. "I'm his sister, Myree. I came down hoping to find him."

"How old are you?" The question came from further back in the crowd, but the mumbling from those closer to her suggested many were thinking the same thing.

"I'm fifteen." She intended to say more but the uproar was instant. It sounded like half the crowd thought she'd just ruined any chance for other jumpers and the other half agreed but wanted them to be quiet so they could ask other questions.

"Kraster's dead, just so you know." Myree searched the faces for the speaker, but now the crowd exploded and Myree joined in demanding details. Was he dead? The crowd didn't seem sure.

She felt a hand on her shoulder and an older man motioned for her to follow. Myree wanted to stay, to get answers, but the man's expression was so calm amid the chaos that she knew her chances were better if she followed. She nudged Ena to get her attention and then they started moving out of the crowd.

"Where are you going?" The crowd wasn't ready to let them go.

"I'm taking them to my house where I can ask her questions in peace and answer her questions the same way. This has been an embarrassment. Everyone cool down and come by my house in an hour. We'll come outside and try this all again." He held up his arms to fend off the backlash. "I know you're upset, but this isn't working and I'm stepping in."

Myree watched him with new interest. He was clearly in charge and his plan made sense. Without waiting for approval or permission, he turned and started walking out of the crowd again. He led them to a small home built at the edge of town. Once inside, he offered them chairs around a carefully polished wooden table in his kitchen and sat down himself. The table was like everything in his house: simple at first glance but very well-made and ornamented with subtle designs on closer examination.

He cleared his throat in what seemed a habit for starting conversations rather than any need. "I'm afraid we've begun horribly today. I understand everyone's frustration but it's no excuse for turning into a mob. Introduction first though; I'm Gren. And did I hear correctly that you're Myree and Ena?" He looked at each of them as he said their names and they both nodded. "It a pleasure to meet you. I was thinking about your question, Myree, as we were walking here. I'll save my questions for later. You want to know about your brother."

"Yes please. Is he really dead? He didn't light a signal fire when he came down."

"Oh, he survived the landing, although it was a horrible crash if I'm remembering correctly. His pair died shortly afterward, I can't remember his name."

"I knew it! I knew he was alive." It hadn't been a mistake to glide down. She'd been suppressing the fear that she was making a horrible mistake, and now that she knew he survived she could acknowledge how girthy the fear had been. "His pair's name was Wilton." Myree croaked out the words, her emotions boiling over.

"That's right. I remember now. Well, Kraster lived just outside Lin until about a year and a half ago. He lived with Cindl on a skinny meadow near the cliffs. The problem is that he left to try going around the mesa, and like everyone else who's ever tried that, he never came back. Most of us think he's dead. I can't think of a delicate way of saying that, I'm afraid."

Myree reviewed Gren's words mentally, looking for a way around them. "He's dead?" It was all she could muster. The news was like water thrown on a raging fire. The fire sputtered and hissed and sent up clouds of steam as it fought to stay alive.

"We don't know for sure, I'll admit, but it's been over a year. I'm sorry Myree. I wish I had better news for you."

Ena jumped in. "You said others have tried too and they never come back?"

"That's right. We're generally safe between the Knife and Echo Canyon, but everyone who tries to explore beyond just disappears. We honestly don't know what happens to them, but they might as well be dead."

"Or captured!" Myree was back. There were tears on her cheeks but the embers were too hot to be doused with one bucket of water.

"Don't get mad. I'm just telling you what everyone else will. When someone disappears, it isn't uncommon for someone to go looking for them. None of them ever return. So yes, maybe they're being held in a prison on the other side of the mesa. I don't know."

"I didn't mean to get mad at you. It's just that everyone's been telling me he's dead ever since he jumped, even though they didn't really know. Now you're doing the same thing."

Gren's face visibly softened. "I can't imagine what you're going through right now. We talk about the people who disappear as being dead partly to discourage others from following them. You must know exactly what I'm talking about."

Myree nodded then dropped her face into her hands. She didn't want to cry but her tears kept coming anyway. If anything, she felt more angry than sad. She'd been right to hope, to risk so much coming down, only to miss him by a year and a half. She wanted to believe he was still alive and hated how quickly everyone assumed the worst. This did feel worse though; it was harder to imagine reasons why he hadn't come back - why everyone who left never came back.

Gren and Ena were quiet, giving her space until she was ready.

"Who was the woman you mentioned, the one he lived with outside of town?"

"Cindl. She was the first person to find him after they crashed out in the forest. It was quite a ways out. I didn't know her before Kraster came down. Before Kraster she lived out on the fringe. This is all second hand, but the story is that she loved a man who she thought loved her back, but he ended up marrying another woman. It's probably true. I can imagine moving out to the fringe if that happened to me."

"What's the fringe?" Ena beat Myree to the question.

"You don't use that term on the mesa? It's hard to keep track, especially when it's been so long since anyone new came down. The fringe just means the area close to the desert. Almost all the humans live within a day's walk of the cliffs, but a few people head farther down. I don't really know where the fringe starts; it mostly just means near the desert and a long way from here. But she's very nice, at least every time I've talked to her. Although, there's something intimidating about her. It's not because she's mean, but you can just tell that she… I don't know exactly. I would say there just seemed to be a fierceness under the surface. Now that I think about it, Kraster was the same way. Maybe that's why they ended up so close. They both seemed kind and dangerous at the same time. Anyway, she looked out for him like she was his mother."

"I'd like to talk to Cindl as soon as possible."

"Oh, you can't do that. She disappeared when he left. She either followed him or went back to the fringe. She didn't say goodbye to anyone so we don't know. Technically, Kraster didn't say goodbye either, but he'd been talking about making the trip for months and asking everyone questions, so when he disappeared, we all just knew where he went."

"I'll bet she went with your brother, don't you think?"

"I hope so. Ena, I'm going to follow him around the mesa. I know he might be dead, but I'm going to look for him. You heard Gren, I probably won't come back. You shouldn't come. He isn't your brother."

"I'm coming. We're in this together, remember?"

"Sorry, I hate to interrupt, but Ena, you should know that larrens will be coming into town to meet you tomorrow. You should expect them to bring you with them when they leave. You seem like very close friends so I thought you should know. The larren and the human always split up after they land. We don't get along as well down here as you do up on the mesa."

"Why not?"

"It's hard to pinpoint why, but we don't trust each other. I have to admit, I usually blame the larrens, but for all I know, they sit around and blame the humans. It's really hard on some of the humans who come down. They're usually friends with the larren they make the jump with and it hurts when their pair becomes distant. I was born down here, so honestly, it's hard for me to imagine having a larren friend."

Ena and Myree looked at each other across the table and the fierceness in their eyes was not under the surface. "I'm staying with Myree. I don't care what everyone else did."

CHAPTER NINETEEN

MIDDLE OF THE NIGHT

GREN'S PREDICTIONS PROVED accurate. The next day, larrens streamed into town to talk to Ena. They had no interest in Myree, but asked Ena to join them at a large meeting so they could all hear her. When she finally returned late that night, Myree had already gone to bed.

"Myree. Wake up. We need to talk."

"I thought you might have left with them."

"No, of course not, but that's what we need to talk about. The larrens down here really don't like humans. It was all I could do to get out of there and come back here tonight. They were pumping me for information about the mesa like you'd expect, but they were also trying to poison my view of humans. I think I was expecting it to be subtle, but it wasn't."

"But why? Why don't they like humans?"

"I don't know, but they're going to keep trying to pull us apart. I think we should leave tonight."

"Right now? It's the middle of the night. I'm tired."

"They'll be back tomorrow. They know you're Kraster's sister and they seem to assume you're going to go around the mesa looking for him. I mean, everyone assumes that. The point is, I'm sure they're going to follow us. Leaving now is probably the best chance we'll ever have of slipping away unnoticed. I really think we should go now."

Myree was still waking up but everything was slowly sinking in. Everyone, humans and larrens, would know she intended to go after Kraster. She'd told Gren as much earlier. If the larrens really didn't like humans down here, then they needed to be careful.

"One more thing, I think the larrens might be responsible for Kraster never coming back. I think we should head away from the cliffs first to throw them off, and then curve back to start following the cliffs around."

"You think they might have hurt my brother?"

"I overheard two of them talking about your brother and I only caught a sliver of the conversation, but they sounded like they knew where he was."

"So he's alive!"

"It was less than a sentence, so I'm nervous to read too much into it, but I think he probably is."

"That's great news!"

"Yes, but it means we have to get away from here now while we can. I know they'll follow us."

"But they might bring me to Kraster. That would be great."

"And they might not. If they decide to capture you, then where you go won't be up to you anymore."

"Okay, let's go. Should we tell Gren?"

"No. Let's just leave him a note."

Myree had spent most of her day gathering supplies for their trip. It had taken all day because there were a million question to answer everywhere she stopped. But she had everything they needed and they were packed in less than half an hour. Ena couldn't fit through the back window, so Myree climbed out and Ena handed her their bags. Myree hid them in the trees behind Gren's house and then went around to see if there was anyone watching the front. Ena was sure someone would be watching the house, and she was right. Next to the house across the street, she could just make out the shape of a large larren sitting back under some small trees. Since Ena would need to leave out the front door, Myree needed to get rid of that larren, at least for a few minutes.

It took fifteen minutes to get there, but Myree had gone the long way around and now crouched in some bushes on the far side of the larren guard. She could see him resting and beyond him was Gren's house, with Ena waiting inside. Her plan was simple; she would start a fire and then throw stones at the house beside the larren. If it worked, whoever lived there would wake up, come out to see who was throwing rocks at their house, and then investigate the fire. The larren guard wouldn't want to be implicated and she guessed he would abandon his post. The risk was that she would get caught, but she couldn't think of a better plan.

She moved farther back into the forest, out of direct sight of the larren or the house and started building her fire. If she did this right, she could start the fire small and get away before it was big enough to attract attention. It was hard finding branches in the dark, but she managed to build a large pile and then started a small fire at one edge. She backed away into the trees watching it carefully to be sure it was building on itself. As soon as she was sure it would keep burning, she crept back into the trees toward her next target. She had five large rocks in her pockets and she pulled out the first two. Then she waited, looking back at the forest for a hint of firelight. It only took a few more minutes until she heard the first crack of burning wood. She knew the larren would have heard that too. It was now or never. She threw the first rock as hard as she could against the back of the house, trying not to hit a window. The stone struck with a loud thud and she could hear the larren sentry start moving. She threw the second and decided that was enough. Inside the house she heard muttering and someone moving. She had to go. She ran as fast as she could behind two more houses, then ran across the street before the angry neighbor came out their front door. Ena was waiting at the back window when Myree got there.

"Quick. Gren's awake; I can hear him."

Across the street, they could hear the neighbor yelling into the darkness. Myree climbed back in through the window and they both came out of their room just as Gren was coming out of his.

"What in the world is going on out there. You two can go back to sleep. I'll see what all the yelling's about."

"We'll at least peek out the door with you. It's an exciting town you've got here."

Gren opened the front door and walked across the street. A few other neighbors were coming out too. You couldn't see the flames behind the house, but you could hear it and see the light reflecting off the leaves. The whole group of them headed back into the trees and Ena and Myree followed at a distance. As soon as they were in the trees, they moved off to the left and started a long slow loop around town and finally back to their bags behind Gren's house. They couldn't hear Gren, so they guessed he wasn't back yet. It was time to go. After all the build-up to get to this point, it was hard to walk away from the safety of Gren's home and the town in general.

Instead of heading parallel to the cliffs toward Echo Canyon, they headed downhill away from the cliffs and then started curving toward The Knife. Myree had mentioned to Gren that she would retrace Kraster's steps, so instead they were going to go around the opposite way. With some luck any attempt to find and follow them would be misdirected for at least a couple of days. It was dark and they didn't want to leave a trail, so they moved very slowly and carefully through the forest until the sky gave its first hints of morning. Then they climbed a small rocky hill, found a spot behind some large boulders that would shield them from view, and fell asleep.

CHAPTER TWENTY
HATRED

THREE MONTHS HAD passed since the Rain Games and the shifts had returned to their digging, but everyone still talked about the final match. No one had seen anything like it and Kraster's name floated through the air more than any other. Even the guards seemed interested and they invited Kraster and Bend to a larren gathering where they could recount the game for all the guards to hear. It was worded as an invitation but there was no way to refuse and Kraster was uncomfortable with the attention. Bend was unusually quiet as they walked to the guard gate at the appointed time.

"It's Kraster and Bend! Welcome! Through here and follow me!" The larren guided them through several more gates and then completely out of the worker's camp. They walked along the outside perimeter and were joined by other guards all moving toward the fire pit. It was in a wide stretch of grass just outside the last wall but before the forest started. The larrens regularly gathered there and the flames were often visible from the camp.

There were already several dozen guards and a fire was

being built. It wasn't dark yet, but the guards often sang and laughed well into the night. They were in a good mood and kept coming up to greet their guests.

Kraster and Bend were led to a log on the edge of the gathering and told to wait until the rest of the guards could make it. Behind them was open grass for about a hundred meters and then the forest. Kraster's mind raced to consider an escape. He was almost sure he and Bend could outrun the larrens, but there might be guards hidden in the trees. Surely they must know how tempting an escape attempt would be. Would Bend come with him? He didn't know. If he didn't, they would probably punish him for Kraster's escape. They'd probably punish Cindl too. But he may never get a better chance for the rest of his life. He knew Cindl would yell at him to go.

Before he could make up his mind he was interrupted. "Hey Kraster, we decided to bring your Mom out too!" Kraster and Cindl had chosen to let the initial misunderstanding persist, and he often thought of her that way anyway. They let go of Cindl's arms and she walked quickly toward them. Her face was hard but Kraster knew her well enough to see the fear. For the first time he realized they were in trouble. How could he have been so naive? Now he understood Bend's silence; he obviously knew, or at least suspected. He still sat quietly staring at the flames.

"Cindl, should we make a run for it?" He resisted the urge to glance over his shoulder at the trees.

"No. This is all a show. They want you to think you might get away. They're hoping you'll try."

"But what if it isn't? This might be our only chance. Shouldn't we try?"

She hesitated and he knew she had considered the same

thing. "Kraster, they're going to beat us; maybe kill us tonight. They won't let us escape."

"How do you know?"

"It's been done before. The others told me as soon as you were taken out here. Ask Bend."

Bend looked up and nodded but remains silent.

The guards kept up the charade. They hauled Kraster in front of the fire and asked him to retell the Rain Game story. Kraster felt like a fool, but he told the story on the small chance Cindl and Bend were wrong. The guards laughed and cheered, and as the story progressed, they cheered a little too loudly. It was becoming clear they were cheering for something else.

"Oh Kraster, what a fantastic story! Thank you. Thank you for sharing it. I have to say, hearing a story like that gets me a little excited. It makes me want to hurt someone!" The guards shouted their approval. "Who should we start with?"

Each of their names could be heard rising and falling above the noise and after several minutes of argument they decided to start with Bend and save Kraster for last. Over the next four hours they were beaten brutally to the sound of wild cheers, songs and a crackling fire. Kraster screamed for them to stop, begged them to leave Bend and Cindl out of this, fought with all his strength, and watched his best friends suffer. As the hours slowly passed his terror changed into hatred: a hatred fiercer than he had ever felt.

The guards left them lying in the grass beside the dying fire until morning, then made them stand and march back to camp in time to join the rest of the Shift Three digging crew that was gathering for the march up the tunnel. No one said a word. The guards struck Cindl again knocking her to the ground. They were hoping to provoke a reaction but everyone knew a reaction would only make things worse for their beaten friends.

Kraster couldn't see. His eyes were swollen shut. He could hardly stand and every breath hurt. Several of his toes and fingers were broken, but he was alive. For a brief moment he was glad he couldn't see Cindl and Bend. The guards forced them to walk to the tunnel entrance on their own strength, but as the darkness enclosed them, their friends gathered to carefully pick them up and carry them the rest of the trip.

CHAPTER TWENTY ONE

TWO OPTIONS

Myree and Ena had been traveling for three nights and the Knife rose up above the trees in front of them. From a distance, and in the daylight, it looked like a giant ax had been swung upwards from below ground, slicing up through the forest and out of the side of the cliff. It started almost half way up the cliffs, jutting out and sloping downward for about three kilometers before ending rather abruptly in a collapsed pile of rock. From the side you couldn't tell it was skinny, but it was clearly steep and it was easy to see how it got its name. They'd been drifting back toward the cliffs as they hiked, subconsciously hoping to avoid the long detour, but now it was obvious they would have to head further out to go around. Myree thought she would be able to climb it, but there was no way Ena could.

The trouble was, they were not alone in the forest. There were larrens out looking for them. The night before, a group of them had set up their camp a stone's throw away from where Myree and Ena were hiding and the conversations they overheard had been terrifying. The larrens were not interested in catching them; they intended to kill them. Both Myree and Ena.

As they hiked through the forest, any little noise would send panic flooding through Myree's mind. She had felt so brave when she decided to make the jump. She knew Kraster might be in danger, but in her imagination, she would be coming down to help him, maybe even save him. She never dreamed she would be hunted and she had never felt so scared. They were almost out of food, but she didn't want to eat anyway.

Now they were trapped. The cliffs rose up on their right, the Knife blocked their path forward, and the larren hunters roamed further out to their left. In theory they could try to retreat back the way they came, but that would just lead them back toward civilization which included larrens.

"Myree, let's set up camp. It could take us awhile to find a really good hiding place before the sun comes up."

"Yeah, okay. We can't go much further anyway; the Knife's really close now."

"I can't see it in this light. You can really see it?"

"Well, sort of. I can't see details, but it is a very different shade than the sky above it."

"I wish larrens could see as well as humans at night. No, I take that back! They probably would've found us by now if we could see better at night. It's our best advantage."

"I suppose, but I get so scared sneaking around in the dark."

Myree looked around them for what seemed like the worst places to hide and then they went to see if there were any hiding places there after all. The hope was that the searching larrens would instinctively look for them in the places that seemed like the best places to hide. So they walked out into the middle of a small meadow and stumbled into a small depression. It wasn't very big, but they decided they could lay down and the grass would hide them. They flattened out the grass at the bottom and tried to lean the grasses on the edges over them to hide any trace of their hiding place. It would be a very hot hiding place during the day if it were the middle of summer, but it should be perfect for a January day. If there wasn't any breeze, they might even be able to take off their coats for awhile. The sun was starting to rise and they settled in, eating a bit of food and preparing to try to sleep.

"Hey Ena."

"Yeah?"

"Once it gets dark again, we're going to have to go toward the hunters."

Ena didn't say anything for a long time. They had both been thinking about it all night.

"I think you should try climbing the Knife, Myree. Hold on! I know what you're going to say, but we both know it's the right thing to do. You could make it over and escape. You could find Kraster. If we try to go around, they're going to find us."

"Ena, I'm not leaving you here by yourself."

"Oh, come on! I don't want us both to die. This way you have a chance. A good chance!"

"I keep thinking about the Sun Pendant. We should try to use it. We'll just walk around during the day until they find us. We could even try to get their attention. Jesh thought it might help."

"No way. We've talked about this. I told them about the pendant at the meeting in town and they all just stared at me. Maybe the King knows about it, but the larrens out here don't.

Besides, even Jesh didn't seem sure it would work. If we were just going to be arrested, then sure, it would be worth the risk, but if they don't know what it is, we're dead."

"We're just running out of better options."

Ena sounded defeated but made another effort. "Look, if I could climb but you couldn't, what would you be suggesting right now?"

"That we stick together and try to go around."

"No you wouldn't! Myree, I know you too well to fall for that. You would be telling me to climb; to save myself."

"Either way, I'm terrified. I wish I could go back. I wish we'd been caught on the mesa. I'd be at home, probably really annoyed, but I'd be safe."

"Me too. I'm sorry I jumped with you. I never should have agreed to this."

"No, it's not your fault. You might die because of me. I feel so dumb for coming down here."

"It's okay. I wanted to come. I should have been smarter about all this too, but I wasn't. Look, you need to do the right thing. The right thing is to get one of us out of this. And since you're the one with the brother to find, it's great news that you're the better climber and can get out of this. Think about it. You know this is the right thing to do."

"No, I don't." Myree's response was barely a whisper. Tears filled her eyes and slipped into the grass as the sum total of all the various fears piled up. Each individual fear layered on top of the other, creating a weight in her mind that was finally too much. It was like a roof collapsing after so much effort to hold it up. She was scared of sneaking around in the dark hoping they didn't walk into a larren campsite; scared that Kraster might be dead anyway and all of this was for nothing. The thought of Ena being alone and hunted scared her. Above all the others, she was terrified of being found and killed herself. She tried not to imagine it, but she couldn't help it.

Her mom would be holding her close; whispering in her ear and smoothing her hair. The thought of her voice and touch was so vivid in her mind, but so impossibly far away. Her throat was so tight it hurt, but finally, sleep pulled her in and gave her a new shelter to hide under for a few hours.

Myree could tell from the light that it must be early afternoon now. There was a gentle breeze, but sunlight filtered through the dry swaying grasses and she felt comfortably warm in her dirty coat. She wasn't slipping back to sleep as quickly anymore and she lay deep in thought. It was very possible that this would be one of the most important decisions she made in her entire life, which was a staggering idea when she thought about how much longer she hoped to live. There were countless ways to think about it, but they all boiled down to two sets of options. Option one

Option one: Stay with Ena like she had promised on the mesa, increasing the likelihood that she would be caught and killed, and lowering the chances of finding and helping her brother. Option two: Abandon Ena to be hunted alone, but lowering the chances of dying as a fifteen-year-old herself, and increasing the chances of finding her brother. She could think of several expressions people used to describe having two bad options, but none of them captured the anguish she felt. The second option made the most sense logically, but she couldn't stand the idea of being a person who would sacrifice a friend because it was logical. This was a decision that would define her, and without realizing it, she had been desperate to figure out who she was.

She had several hours left to decide, but she already knew. She was going to stay with Ena like she had promised and face the danger. There hadn't been a single moment in time when she made the decision; it was more like that choice had settled into place as the options bounced around in her mind. The other set of options just didn't fit. She knew everything would feel crazy again after dark, but lying here in the grass, she was happy. For the first time in her life, Myree had a handhold on who she was and it felt really good. She could be terrified, but not give in to fear. And she kept her promises.

CHAPTER TWENTY TWO

GLOBELIGHT FIGHT

THE SKY WAS clear and the stars gave just enough light to let them creep through the forest. Somewhere off to their right was the campfire that had forced them to detour. It was unusual to see a campfire this late. Based on what they had overheard a few nights earlier, the larrens were generally trying to find them during the day and being as quiet and inconspicuous as possible at night in the hope that Myree and Ena would stumble onto them. So a campfire didn't really fit that strategy. But there it was, clearly visible through the trees. There was nothing to do but go around. If they moved closer to investigate, Myree's night vision advantage would disappear. And so the only decision had been, left away from the Knife, or right toward the Knife. The possibility that it was somehow a trap danced at the edge of their minds, and they decided to go left - away from where they would have liked to go. They couldn't see the fire through the trees anymore but Myree guessed it must be directly to their right by now, or even a little behind them. She could feel herself relaxing and forced herself to stay alert. Had she been floating high above the trees she would have seen that there were fifteen campfires spread out in a line through the forest. It was an old trick the larrens had developed to catch humans at night. They knew they couldn't see as well so they spread themselves out in the gaps between the fires and sat quietly to listen. They hoped Myree and Ena would see one of the fires and try to sneak around it in the darkness. Even though the larrens were spread out from each other, because they only had to fill in the dark gaps between the campfires, they could extend their trap much farther.

Myree was leading Ena carefully through the forest, trying to avoid anything that would make noise or that would leave evidence they had passed through. They knew the larrens would be out hunting for them at sunrise and a trail could lead them straight to the next hiding place.

Just ahead, Myree heard a noise and then a globelight materialized in the air. After straining to see in the darkness, the globelight was blindingly bright. She froze, trying to figure out what was going on. As her eyes adjusted, Myree saw a larren holding the globelight high in the air with one hand and an empty bag in the other. A split second after Myree could focus on him, he could focus on her and their eyes locked. The larren yelled and ran toward them. In the same amount of time, Myree understood that she had to smash that globelight if they were going to have any chance of escape. She had taken a few instinctive steps backwards but now she stopped and sprinted toward the larren at full speed. The larren had clearly expected them to turn and run, so although there was nothing very threatening about a fifteen-year-old girl rushing him, he pulled to a stop in surprise. Myree closed the distance fast and dove for the globelight. By the time the larren realized what she was trying to do, she had her hands on it. Instead of fighting each other they fought to pull the globelight from each other's grip. The larren was much stronger, but Myree was fighting for her life, and their battle was an explosion of intensity.

Ena had just started to run away when she saw Myree stop out of the corner of her eye. She didn't react as quickly as Myree and by the time she had recovered from her shock, Myree had slammed into the larren. What was she thinking? Then she understood too. They had to get away from this larren as quickly as possible and their only real chance to do that was in the dark. The larren guard was becoming increasingly desperate to regain the advantage. Without letting go of the globelight, he was throwing Myree back and forth against a tree trunk, trying to hurt her as much as he could. But Myree wouldn't let go.

Ena turned and charged the larren who was so focused on the globelight that he never saw her coming. She jumped and smashed her shoulder into the side of his head. Both Myree and the larren fell to the ground, but the guard was dazed from the blow and Myree was left holding the globelight.

"We have to break it! We need something hard to smash it on!" Myree threw the globelight as hard as she could at the root of the tree but it just bounced off and rolled to their right. The larren was starting to mumble and tried to get up. Even worse, they could hear other larrens coming from both sides, yelling to their friend. If they got here with their globelights it was over.

"Here! Myree, over here! Here's a rock."

Myree rushed over and threw the globelight down on the rock which was just barely sticking out above the leaves and dirt. It cracked and started to leak but didn't shatter.

"Again! Don't get any on your hands; they might glow in the dark."

Myree didn't have time to be careful. She picked it up and threw it again at the rock. This time it broke open and the glowing liquid spilled out onto the dirt. The larren was standing up now and moving toward them. He was still unsteady but his head was clearing. Myree looked down at her hands which were glowing and starting to itch. For the second time, she charged the larren and smeared the glowing liquid on his face, trying to get it as close to his eyes as she could. He tried to grab her but she jumped out of his reach just in time.

"Myree, we have to go now!" The other larrens were getting closer, they probably only had a minute head start. "Your hands! You have to hide them. Can you put them in your pockets?"

"Yeah, I'll try. Let's go. Tell me if you can still see them."

They ran off through the trees going as fast as they could to take advantage of their small head start. The larren behind them tried to follow, but the glowing liquid around his eyes made it impossible to see where he was going.

"Am I still glowing?"

"I can't see your hands but it looks like some of it splattered on your coat. I'll try to clean it off later, but we can't stop now."

They ran as fast as they could without worrying about leaving a trail. They would worry about that later. They could hear the larrens behind them yelling and occasionally breaking a branch, but as they ran, the pursuers faded behind them. An hour later, they finally stopped for a short break. Myree's hands were burning now and she tried rubbing them in the dirt and against a tree, but nothing helped. Her whole body ached and she could tell she was bleeding from several places, including her face, but it was too dark to investigate. After each taking a drink, Ena poured the rest of their water on Myree's hands trying to wash them off without much success. Neither of them knew what was in a globelight but in a feeble attempt at humor, they both vowed never to touch the stuff again.

"Okay, we have to keep going."

"Are you sure Myree? I think you need to rest."

"No, I'd rather be running to distract myself anyway. Can you keep going?"

"Yeah. For now, anyway."

They resumed their run, moving a bit slower this time. Myree was making more of an effort to avoid leaving a trail now that they had a significant head start. Finally, two hours later, they came to a river. Myree washed her hands properly and was able to get most of the liquid off, although she thought some of it must have seeped into her skin. The water was almost unbearably cold, but they decided to try drifting down the river for a while despite the risk of rapids or waterfalls. They didn't have much darkness left, and it was the best way they could think of to put distance between them and their hunters. More importantly, it would give them a fresh start somewhere on the opposite bank to strike out carefully without leaving a trail.

As the sun came up, they climbed out of the water, shaking with cold but forcing themselves to hike into the forest. They found a hollow between three large trees and huddled together under a blanket of leaves. It took a long time to fall asleep.

CHAPTER TWENTY THREE

A KIND MASTER

Ena stood at the door of the small cottage. She had to knock to save their lives, but this was surrender, and even now on the verge of starvation her mind searched for another way. There was nothing left to do. Myree had finally collapsed half an hour ago and Ena knew she wouldn't last much longer herself. They just couldn't find enough food and after three months of trekking and cool winter nights, it had finally hit a critical point. Ena dropped her head and closed her eyes to physically accept defeat. Then she opened them, tried to steady herself, and knocked on the door. A moment later, a young woman opened the door and put her hand to her mouth when she saw Ena.

"You're human! I'm so glad. My friend and I are starving and the larrens are trying to catch us and kill us. Would you please help us? My friend is back in the forest that way." Ena pointed back the way she'd come.

"Tema, come quick! There's a larren at the door and I think it's Ena!"

The woman knew her name. Ena thought about running,

but she wouldn't get very far. An old larren came slowly to the door and stood beside the human. She stared at Ena and a smile spread across her face.

"Ena, tell me where Myree is."

Ena could feel the last of her strength and hope ebbing away. "Never."

The next time Ena opened her eyes, someone was trying to spoon something into her mouth. She spit it out and tried to resist, but the voice was soothing, and she didn't have the energy to fight. Whatever it was tasted delicious. Besides, she wasn't dead. That was good. Maybe it wasn't poison. She allowed the spoon into her mouth and swallowed the warm broth. Her eyes finally focused and she recognized the woman from the doorway.

"You're safe. And don't worry, we found Myree. Most of us thought you were both dead out there. The resistance has been looking for you too, but King Marik's guards are everywhere. We have so many questions, but Tema thinks we should wait until tomorrow - let you regain some strength."

"It's okay, I can talk a little."

"Are you sure?"

"Yeah. I have questions too."

"Hold on, I'll get Tema."

"Wait, is Myree okay?"

"Yes, she's in the next room. She's weaker than you, but I think she'll be fine."

"I knew she was giving me too much of the food. She said I was bigger." The woman's smile was so big and beautiful that Ena caught herself smiling too.

"I don't think you need to feel bad about that. It's just been harder to get food down her throat. When you would wake up enough you'd spit it out, but we usually could get you to swallow quite a bit before that happened. Don't worry about Myree, it's taking a little longer, but we're taking good care of her."

The woman gave Ena one more spoonful of broth, set the bowl on the floor and rose to leave the room. Just before she got to the doorway she turned back toward Ena. "You can trust Tema. I understand that you don't trust larrens down here, but Tema is one of the good ones. She moved out here with me so she wouldn't have to pretend I was her slave anymore. I don't know if that makes any sense to you, but it's the most important thing in the world to me." She smiled again and Ena noticed the tears forming in the corners of her eyes. "And, thanks for protecting Myree."

She walked out of the room and Ena stared at the empty doorway trying to process everything she'd just heard. She had just met a slave for the first time, or at least someone who had been a slave at some point. Tema was old enough that she moved slowly, and Ena heard her coming before she saw her. Her fur was a mix of very light brown and white, and although she smiled, Ena sensed this was a face that didn't always express the mind behind it.

"Good morning, Ena. I hear you have some questions for me?" Her voice was steady and quiet with a touch of raspiness.

"Why were those larrens trying to kill us?" Ena didn't think it was a complicated question, but Tema looked perplexed.

"Finding the way down to the root answer can be so difficult. The obvious answer is that King Marik despises humans. I don't know that he hates them, he just looks down on them - thinks they're worthy to be our slaves but nothing more. If you pushed me to go a level deeper I'm not sure I could answer.

Why does King Marik despise humans? That's the real question. But King Marik is simply the latest king to hold such a view. It's so deeply woven into our past that I can't think of a way to pull it out in a neat answer. I see your eyes glazing over! The short version is that King Marik has a long-standing rule that any humans who wander out of the restricted area should be killed. Normally, the guards wouldn't have been trying to kill you too, but you're the first larren anyone can remember that chose to stick with their pair after gliding down. That couldn't be left unchecked."

"I still can't believe I'm the only larren to do that."

"You are. At least in hundreds of years. Oh, plenty of larrens feel horrible about deserting their friends, but they're convinced to do it anyway. I did. Almost a hundred years ago now, but I left Thord in the restricted area. I'm sure he's been dead for twenty years, but I still think about that decision. We're all pressured to do it and everyone but you gave in. And then, as if to poke your finger in King Marik's eye, you attacked one of his guards to protect your human friend!"

"How do you know about that?"

"Oh, now that's the funny part. The larren you and Myree fought made the mistake of telling his comrades what happened. Needless to say, he's been ridiculed constantly ever since. I'm sure he's lost his job, maybe his life. I suppose that part isn't funny. As you might guess, the story that a human girl dared to attack a full grown larren guard and that you, Ena, rushed to her aid - well, that's the kind of story that sweeps from cliff to fringe. Everyone knows your names, and King Marik is desperate to have you both dead."

Ena could feel hope unfurling in her mind. "You're not going to turn us in are you?"

"No, my dear. You found my house. Of all the houses! I'm part of the resistance and I will not turn you over to the King."

"A resistance against King Marik?"

"That's one part of it, but only because we don't think King Marik will change. What really defines us is our belief that slavery is morally wrong. For now, we keep ourselves secret. I mean, everyone knows that there is a resistance, but they don't know who's in it. Someday, we'll be strong enough to get rid of King Marik and make a new start."

"That woman - was she your slave?"

"Sadly yes. I try not to treat her like a slave but according to our laws and customs, she still is."

"If you treat her so well, it doesn't seem so bad. She seems to really love you."

"If the master is kind maybe slavery isn't so bad, right? You're not the first to think so, but respectfully, I strongly disagree. The kindness or cruelty of the master doesn't determine whether slavery is right or wrong. I'm getting older and my mind is still sharp, but what if, in another thirty years, I change my mind and start treating her like my slave again? I could have her killed because she displeased me. All these years of kindness don't change the fact that I own her. No, we shouldn't own another self-aware being, no matter how different they are from us."

"Why don't you let her go?"

"There's nowhere for her to go. As you've just experienced, getting to and from the restricted zone is very difficult. I would have said impossible yesterday, but here you are. Someday, before she dies, I'm going to set her free. It feels impossible some days, but that's the dream that drives me to keep building this resistance."

Ena was almost sure she knew the answer but she had to ask. "Do you happen to know if Myree's brother made it through from the restricted zone? His name was Kraster."

"Indeed he did! Another small miracle. Our sources discovered that he was sent to work on the tunnel."

"He's alive!"

"We think he is. We're still trying to get a message to him, but we don't have much of a network among the tunnel guards. As far as we can tell, he's in there."

"Kraster's a slave?"

"Yes, I'm afraid so. All the humans you meet over here are slaves."

"Does Myree know?"

"Not yet. She's only opened her eyes a few times and never long enough to have a conversation."

"She'll be so happy he's alive! Maybe this was all worth it. Will you help us get to the tunnel? I know Myree will want to go."

"What will you do when you get there?"

"I don't know exactly. But I know Myree will try to save him and I know I'll help her."

"Well, I don't want to promise anything before I've had time to consider it, but I will consider it. I had a few questions for you too, but I can see you're getting tired again, and my questions can wait. I'm proud to know you, Ena."

CHAPTER TWENTY FOUR

SABOTAGE

"Cindl. Hey, I guess this is goodbye. I'm heading back in."

"Kraster, I'm having second thoughts. I don't think you should do this. We might be able to escape. We should be patient."

"No, I need to do this. I'm the only person they'll let in there from second shift and if we wait to tell the next shift, we'll have dug too far past it; they won't let us go back and explore old caves. This might be our only shot at really hitting them hard. They've been digging this tunnel for five hundred years."

"I know, I know. I just don't want you to do it."

"Hey, don't cry! The guards will see you."

"Kraster, don't do this."

"We're slaves, Cindl! I hate it. I don't want to dig a tunnel for the rest of my life - especially one that will let these larrens reach the humans on the mesa. I'm probably going to die in this tunnel one way or the other. But this way, I can really hurt them. Would you do this if they would let you in the cave?"

Cindl didn't answer but reached out and gripped Kraster's hand. She would have hugged him, but that would have attracted too much attention.

"Ever since the day I found you in the forest, seven, almost eight years ago, I've been amazed at your courage. I know I'm not your real Mom, but..."

"Cindl, don't. I can't cry right now."

"Well, I love you Kraster."

"I love you too."

They both threw themselves into the digging for several minutes to let the quiet tears run themselves out, then Kraster turned and walked toward the cave opening, grabbed his creeper bag, and climbed in.

He moved quickly through the large passageway he had found the day before. Within five minutes he was at the bottom of the vertical shaft. It was like a narrow cliff inside the mesa, and as he had done the day before, he climbed to the top and then continued to follow the cave further upward through the rock. He caught the first sounds of water just around the sharp left turn. The sound became louder and louder until he came to the edge of the underground river.

His first task was to clear the boulder field between the river and the cave entrance he had just come through. It was really a two-person job, but there was no one to help him. He rolled the largest boulders to the side and then used a small hand shovel he'd smuggled into his bag to dig out the smaller rocks. He smiled imagining the old version of himself trying to do this work. Almost two years in the tunnels had hardened him and he was proud of his strength and stamina. But finally, even he collapsed to rest. He was almost completely healed from the beating but his left shoulder ached more than it would have before. A few more large stones and a tiny portion of the river would flow down through the cave, over the narrow cliff, and out into the main tunnel. At least he hoped it would. That was the signal they had agreed on. He wasn't sure it would work, but if it did, it would give his friends time to revolt and race down the tunnel before the bigger flood.

He reached into his pack and pulled out some food. Their closest friends had all donated their rations to him after breakfast. Not everyone knew what he was doing. They had to assume there were some spies.

He moved his pack up to a ledge near the top of the cave, then dug out the last of the stones to start a stream flowing in a new direction. Then he kept digging to increase the flow of water heading down toward the main tunnel. This was only the first stage of the plan, getting most of the river to flow down the side tunnel would require a lot more work. He carefully walked through the new stream back to the drop to make sure it was flowing over. As he had feared, the waterfall he created ran straight down the climbing route he'd used to get up. There was no way to climb down and be absolutely sure the water was flowing into the main tunnel. But he had checked everywhere the day before and it didn't seem like there was anywhere else for the water to go. He tried listening for any sounds of fighting or running, but the small waterfall was loud enough that it drowned out any noise. There was nothing to do but wait and hope his friends were running down the tunnels before he unleashed the full flood.

Cindl thought that in a panic, they could race to the bottom entrance in six hours; maybe even faster. It had never been attempted. They settled on seven hours to be safe, but they hadn't been able to find a watch so it was all going to be guesswork anyway. Either way, Kraster had some time. The best way to use it would be to sleep, but he was too tense and kept thinking about the boulder he had to move. Finally, he got up and decided to start the prep work.

The boulder was just downstream, and it was massive. This boulder was what triggered the whole idea when he saw it yesterday. It had fallen from the ceiling and was dangerously close to falling into the river. If he could roll it over the edge, it was big enough that he thought it would block most of the river's flow.

For now, he worked on digging out as much debris as possible that might prevent the boulder from rolling in. As he worked it became clear that there hadn't been time to sleep anyway. The work was slow, especially because he was trying to save as much of the rock as he could for later. So rather than just pry up rocks and push them in the river, he pried them up and carried them upstream for later use.

Finally, the prep work was done. The hardest part was still to come, but his stomach growled for food. His first globe light was fading but rather than shake it and waste light, he sat and ate in near darkness. It must be about time. Without a watch, all he could do was imagine himself racing down the tunnel, but he knew he'd lost track of time.

There was a narrow space between the boulder and the outside edge of the cave. He found a rock that just fit in the space near the top and wedged it in. Then he climbed on top of the boulder, leaned against the outside wall and pushed on the boulder with his legs. Nothing happened. He climbed down to see if there was anything else he could dig out of the way, but he'd done all he could. This was going to be about brute strength. He found a slightly better spot to lean against the outside wall, then pushed with every muscle fiber in his body. The boulder shifted a few centimeters and the rock he had placed earlier dropped into the widened space keeping it from rolling back. This was going to work! He pushed again and the rock dropped further. He climbed down and found a larger stone to start at the top of the gap.

His legs trembled as he pushed them past anything he had ever demanded of them. His body pleaded to rest, but he imagined larrens reaching the mesa and making Myree and his parents slaves. It would never happen! He lifted the biggest rock he could carry up onto the boulder to keep the gap widening and then went back to work with his legs.

Finally, he could tell he had crossed some tipping point and the boulder became much easier to move. He prepared himself for the fall and gave the final push sending the boulder crashing into the river. Kraster fell into the depression where the boulder had just been but managed to land on his feet. The force of the water started to roll the boulder downstream and for a moment it looked like it would just be swept away, but then it stopped and never moved again. The river level rose quickly and was soon pouring over the embankment and down the side cave toward the larren's tunnel! Kraster collapsed onto his back with his triumphant yells echoing off the walls.

He closed his eyes and tried to imagine the water pouring out of the cave and rushing down the tunnel. There was enough water from this river that it would be impossible to get back up to the head of the tunnel. He had just sabotaged a five-hundred-year project and he'd protected his family from these terrible larrens.

Every muscle wanted to rest and his mind wanted to shut down, but he forced himself to stand up. Starting with the biggest ones, he rolled smaller boulders into the river, then stones that he could barely lift off the ground, then smaller stones. He hoped they would lodge in gaps around the large boulder and it seemed to work. The river level rose sending even more water down the side cave.

It was done. He laid down again where the boulder had been a few hours ago and fell asleep for a long time.

CHAPTER TWENTY FIVE
SINKING

Myree was doing much better. She was still weak, but it was the awkward phase of any recovery. Sitting around all day felt lazy, but she tired out quickly when helping out around the house. And she was getting anxious to do something about Kraster. Tema assured her that the resistance was weighing its options and that mounting a rescue attempt was being seriously considered. But weeks kept passing and there was no word on a decision.

"Myree, look. Tema's coming." Ena was stretched out on the grass beside Myree enjoying the mid-afternoon sun. Tema rarely came outside so they guessed this must be important.

"Good afternoon Myree; Ena."

"Good afternoon. Any news from the resistance?"

"Bad news I'm afraid. We're still trying to piece together all the details, but there was an incident at the tunnel early this morning. The slaves digging the tunnel apparently diverted an underground river into the tunnel. Everyone's scrambling to think of ways to salvage it, but it looks like the slaves just ruined a 500-year-old project. There's too much water coming down for anyone to move up the tunnel so I think the digging has to stop. Like I said, they're trying to figure out how to save it, but it doesn't look promising."

"That sounds like great news. What am I missing?"

"Well, your brother, Kraster, is the one who figured out how to divert the river, but he had to sacrifice himself to do it. He's the only one that didn't make it out of the tunnel. I'm so sorry Myree. We hadn't been able to get a message to him yet. I'm sure he wouldn't have done it if he'd known how close you were."

The final sentences hardly even registered in Myree's mind. She stood up automatically, staring blankly at Tema. Ena was saying something but she couldn't focus on the words. Then she sank back to her knees and slowly crumpled into a ball on the ground. Finally, the sobs stole her breath away and rocked her body. She could feel Ena beside her and felt a large larren teardrop fall on her forehead.

CHAPTER TWENTY SIX

PROPOSITION

LATER THAT AFTERNOON, Tema invited Ena to go for a walk. Myree had asked to be alone and was in the house. The sun was getting low and Ena guessed they only had about an hour before sunset. They followed a well-worn trail into the forest which was cool and quiet. It was early May and every break in the trees revealed a patch of flowers where enough sunlight could reach the ground. It almost never got cold enough to freeze on the base, but spring was still the most beautiful season.

"Ena, I want to give you a short history. I'm about to ask you to take a big risk, and I think it will help if you know how we got here. Judging from our prior conversations, is it fair to say you don't know about the Cliff War?"

"This is the first I've heard of it."

"I thought as much. Just over five hundred years ago the larrens and humans fought a terrible and vicious war. Both the larrens and humans did things that should never be done, but most of us agree, our side was worse. The war was at a stalemate and we decided we needed help from the mesa larrens.

When we captured humans we would separate the children and force them to climb the cliffs with a plea for help written in the old larren language. No good records were kept, but it's estimated we sent over a thousand children to their death on those cliffs." Ena followed Tema's gaze and saw the cliffs in a new light. They were no longer just beautiful.

"How can I not have heard about this?"

"That's a question I would love to have answered. Our stories indicate that some of those children found a route up the cliffs, and Myree's account of the Crimson Room confirms it. Yet no one who glides down from the mesa, human or larren, has ever heard anything about it. It's hard to understand how that can be possible. We sent some scouts to look for the climbing route where Myree said it should be and they found the natural archway. But I'm getting side-tracked. That's a mystery for today; I wanted to help you understand our history.

"We won the Cliff War. Every human down here was either killed or chased into the desert. Any human you meet now came from the mesa or is the descendant of someone who did. Although that war was five hundred years ago, we continue to see humans as enemies."

"You keep saying we, but neither of us feel that way."

"You're right." Tema stopped walking and looked up at the colored sky to think. "I think I speak that way because it motivates me. I'm a larren, and as a group, larrens continue to treat humans as little more than animals. I'm so ashamed of this. Saying it out loud is difficult. By associating myself with the guilt, at least grammatically, it spurs me to fix it; to risk my life by being part of the resistance. Larrens are committing this evil and larrens should be able to stop it."

"I still don't like it. I don't want to be linked to that way of thinking."

"I know you don't and I love hearing you say that. So let me fast forward to the current situation. You remember hearing about Kraster's friend Cindl?"

"Sure."

"We received word that they're marching her to Rreker this evening. She was very close to Kraster and the King wants to interrogate her. You can probably guess this as well as I can, but we don't think she will be treated kindly."

"Can we intercept her?"

"No, we didn't find out in time and we don't have enough resistance nearby to attempt a rescue anyway. She's heavily guarded. Besides, she's probably almost there by now. But I have an idea for a way you might be able to rescue her. You're one of the only ones who can. We need a larren who can still glide, and second, if you rescue a second human, you will become a symbol for everything the resistance stands for."

"There have to be other young larrens around here that could do it. I'm not saying I won't, but I don't understand."

"Larren pods very rarely hatch down here and the stream of young larrens gliding down ended with Kraster and Wilton. Roughly eight hundred fifty years ago, long before the Cliff War, larrens would walk up to the mesa to deposit our pods in the colder air. There was a narrow ridge called the Finger that connected the mesa to the Tail. The Finger collapsed in an earthquake stranding a group of humans and larrens on the mesa. We've been separated ever since. The hope was that in another five hundred years, the tunnel project would finally reach the top of the mesa and life could return to the way it was. I think I understand why Kraster destroyed it, but I'm still in mourning."

"You support the tunnel project?"

"You're surprised. Yes, I supported the tunnel project. Not the way it was run, using slaves, but the basic idea was wonderful."

"I'm having a hard time separating the idea from the slaves."

"It's probably easier for me because I saw the value of the tunnel project before I was old enough to reject slavery. Well, I guess that's it. You know the most important parts of our sad history. Are you ready to hear how we think you can rescue Cindl from under the king's nose?"

"I'm ready."

CHAPTER TWENTY SEVEN
GOING-AWAY PRESENT

THREE HOURS LATER, Ena ascended the dark stairway up into the human jail tower in King Marik's palace. She was trying to act like this was all normal, but she hadn't been this scared since she and Myree were being hunted. Now she was voluntarily walking into the hunter's lodge hoping that no one would recognize her - that no one would even begin to imagine she might be there. Tema presented the idea with such calm that Ena hadn't guessed at the urgency of it all. As soon as she agreed, they had started walking to Rreker, without even going back to the house first. It was all a little too abrupt and Ena struggled to accept that it was happening. So she blindly followed her guide up the stairs toward Cindl's cell. Her guide had not offered his name, but another guard had greeted him as Dizer. If he was scared, he hid it perfectly. Perhaps because of her own fear, she suddenly realized how much risk members of the resistance had to live with daily. It helped to remember she wasn't the only one taking a risk. When they entered the palace he had joked around with the other guards, introduced Ena as a new trainee named Nari, and led them through the maze of doorways and passageways until they reached the staircase up to the human jail.

At the top, Dizer chatted with the guards on duty. He told Ena to wander around and get familiar with the jail since she would be stationed there for the next month. There wasn't much to the jail. Four cells on two levels, with a narrow stairway between the upper and lower floor right in the middle. Each cell was small and designed for human prisoners. There was only one prisoner at the moment and that was Cindl. So while Dizer was chatting with the guards, she approached Cindl's cell.

"Cindl. Are you awake? Shhhh. Whisper."

"I'm awake. What do you want?"

"I'm here to try to get you out of jail. Kraster's sister Myree is my best friend."

"Myree's down here too? Oh, no."

"Yeah, we came down to look for Kraster. We know he died, and we know you were a good friend to him. So I can't promise this will work, but if you're willing, I'm going to try to rescue you tonight before they bring you to King Marik tomorrow."

"Yes! Thank you. Get me out of here."

"Okay, just sit tight for now, but be ready when I come back."

In total, the human jail had four guards. Two at the top of the tower guarding the cells themselves, and two at the bottom guarding the doorway to the staircase. It was one thing to hear the jail described, but quite another to actually be there. Her mind raced to consider all the things that she was now sure would go wrong.

Dizer said his goodbye and told her to stay out of the way

for the first few days. Then he disappeared down into the dark stairwell. The guards clearly liked him but were not excited about having a new trainee getting in their way. So far so good. Ena found a spot on the top floor that was out of the way and sat down to wait.

The wait was hard. She kept second guessing every decision. Mostly the decision to head to Rreker without saying goodbye to Myree. Tema was right; Myree would have protested, but if she died tonight Myree would lose her brother and best friend in less than a month. She'd be devastated. But whatever the outcome tonight, the only thing left for Myree was to try the old climbing route and go home. She wasn't sure if Myree realized that yet, but she would. Rescuing Kraster's friend was like a going-away present.

There was a lamp on each floor but both guards were down on the lower floor talking and laughing about things she couldn't quite hear. She tried to get comfortable; not knowing how long shc would havc to wait. Every now and then she would glance over at the cell, but Cindl wasn't at the bars and the lamp light was dim anyway. What was taking so long? She only had to wait a few more minutes before the chaos broke. A bell rang out in the night air - four strikes, then a pause, then four more.

"Hey, that's the signal for fire!"

"We need to get out of here! If the fire gets to the tower doors, we're trapped."

"Do we bring the prisoner?"

"No way, let her burn. We'll still be on guard, just at the bottom."

"Hey kid, there's a fire in the palace. We're heading down, you better follow us."

"Okay, I'm coming."

The guards started running down the stairs and Ena noisily stumbled down the stairs from the upper floor to the lower floor, but then she stopped to see if the guards were really gone. Their footfalls echoed up through the open door and Ena fought to stay calm. She walked to the door, closed it and bolted it shut. That was it, she was committed. The keys for the cell doors were hanging beside the door just like Dizer said they would. Ena grabbed them all and ran back up to Cindl's cell.

"There isn't really a fire is there?"

"I think there is. At least there's supposed to be a real fire. Come on, we need to move fast just in case the guards come back soon."

"So what's your plan? I'm in pretty bad shape, I won't be much help trying to fight off anyone at the bottom."

"Well, let's skip the stairs then, what do you say? Follow me."

"I'm starting to get a little nervous that you intend to jump."

"Well, that's the grand plan. I just came down with Myree a few months ago so I can still glide."

"That's great, but I'm not a kid anymore as you may have noticed."

"I know. We aren't sure this will work, but it was the only plan we could think of that was worth trying. So first of all, you're pretty light for an adult human. You aren't very big to start with, and you've been working in the tunnel for several years."

"Well, that's true. Okay, what is second thing?"

"Actually, that was it. I decided I was willing to take the risk to save you. Are you willing to make the jump with me?"

Cindl looked around at the prison cells, weighing her options. "I don't think you've left me much of a choice. If there is a fire, we might be trapped up here. And if there isn't a fire and the guards come back, they're going to be very suspicious that you didn't come with them. I would just get you in trouble."

Ena grinned. "Is that a yes?"

"I suppose it is."

"Here, help me get this door open to the roof. I don't think it's been opened in ages and it's stuck."

Cindl and Ena forced the door open and felt the cool spring air rush in. The first challenge was to get to the other side of the roof. The pitch was too steep to walk on, but there was a narrow ledge that curved out of sight right at the edge. It was enough. Ena had brought a rope and they tied it around themselves to keep Cindl firmly in place on Ena's back. There was nothing left but to make the jump and hope it worked.

"Where are we headed?"

"See that shorter tower over there; almost straight south?"

"Yeah."

"We're going to try to glide to the left of that tower, over the city wall, over those trees and into the clearing on the other side. The resistance is supposed to have a fire lit in the center of the clearing. If we can make it that far, we are in good shape. Actually, there it is, I can see the fire."

"I see it too. Let's go."

"One last thing, if you notice I'm getting off track let me know. Otherwise, try to be quiet when we jump. Hopefully, no one will see us or hear us."

"Got it."

Despite the warning it was hard not to shriek with fear and excitement jumping off the roof. It took a long second of falling before they were going fast enough to glide. That had been true jumping off the mesa too, but in that case there were several kilometers of space below you. This was completely different. The ground raced up at them, but Ena quickly flattened out, adjusted their course and headed toward the left side of the tower. The city wall slipped underneath them and the trees loomed ahead. Cindl instinctively pushed down on Ena's arms at the same time that Ena realized they were not going to clear the trees.

"Right! Go right! There's a gap!"

"Where?"

"There! Straight ahead now."

"That's not a gap!"

"I think we can make it!"

It wasn't a gap as much as a section where the trees were less thick. At the last moment, Ena tucked her arms back and tore through the branches. She intended to try to spread them out on the other side to attempt a landing, but the branches knocked her unconscious. They hit the ground in the clearing and tumbled until the trees on the far side stopped them.

There was no time to let them recover where they lay. Myree and the larren rebels picked up Cindl and Ena as carefully as they could, and then moved into the forest. They marched through the darkness for what felt like days but was more like three hours. Finally, they stopped in a small clearing for about thirty minutes while one larren disappeared off to the right to make sure the hiding place was unwatched. When he returned with a positive report, all but four of the larrens marched off again in roughly the same direction they had been going. The four remaining larrens and Myree carried their injured friends off to the right toward the hiding place. They followed a hard-packed dirt path, moving slowly to avoid leaving a trail that might attract attention away from the larger group that was now just a decoy.

They skipped the large old house that was crowded by the encroaching forest and went around to one of several low-roofed structures built in a row. Myree couldn't tell in the dark, but the building on the far left was different than the rest. It was built against the hillside and was a bit larger. It had been built over an old cave entrance and once the door to the building was closed behind them, they shook on a couple more lights and disappeared into the cave. The natural cave walls eventually ended and were replaced by a larren-made tunnel that had been dug centuries before. It opened into a larger room that would be their home for the next several days while Ena and Cindl recovered from their injuries.

CHAPTER TWENTY EIGHT

DAYLIGHT AND DARKNESS

KRASTER WOKE UP stiff and sore. Moving that boulder had been hard, and his sore muscles served as a badge of honor. A wave of thoughts rushed through his mind Was Cindl dead? Had she and the others made it out of the tunnel? Had the plan worked at all? What if the river flowed somewhere else and the larrens were still happily forcing his friends to dig the tunnel today? He was free! He was not a slave today. He was alone in a cave in the middle of the mesa and would probably die there. How much food did he have? How long could he survive? Where did the old river go?

It was the last question that focused his thoughts. He pulled out one of his globelights and gently shook it. A dim light danced out between his fingers and illuminated the cave around him. If he was racing a clock it was against his lights going out. He was filled with an overwhelming urge to see daylight and he grabbed his pack and started picking his way down the old riverbed. There was still a small stream where the river had once rushed and he realized this was a very good thing. He took a long drink and tried to remember how long a person could survive if they had water. It was weeks not days, but he couldn't remember specifically.

The cave jogged back and forth, occasionally dropped precipitously, and then it stopped at a wide cavern filled by a large underground lake. He had waded through several pools earlier, but this one stretched beyond the reach of his light and was too deep for wading. Kraster carefully sorted through his pack, taking out everything except his last two globelights and his food. He didn't know if the food would survive the swim, so he ate as much as he could and wrapped the remnants tightly. Maybe some would still be in there at the end. He had been swimming hundreds of times, but this was different. He couldn't pinpoint the cause, but he had to force himself to push out into the water. His mind craved a foothold in the near-darkness, but there was only one direction he could go so he willed his mind to focus on smooth steady stokes. There was a noticeable current that helped his progress, but as the minutes passed, it also eliminated the possibility of ever swimming back to where he started. At several points during the swim he had to float on his back with barely enough room between the water and the ceiling of the cave to breathe. The ceiling was smooth, so he guessed that before he dammed the river, this section would have been impassible. Finally, the lake ended in a slippery mound of boulders and he could start walking again. He hiked until his globe light was getting dim and he was getting tired. Then, instead of shaking it for more light, he slept for a while.

He woke up hours later and resumed his trek. He had no sense of direction other than gradually lower. It bothered him that he didn't know whether it was day or night outside. As much as he tried to just hike until he was tired, it all felt wrong. He climbed and marched for what felt like a full day, always glancing up in hope of seeing light. The globelight he carried was getting dimmer and he knew it was about spent. He had one left, but even it wouldn't be very bright at this point. It had been bouncing around in his bag for days now too, but it probably had a little more light left. Still, he was exhausted and he slept deeply.

When he woke up, he ate the last of his food. It had become a sticky mush, but he wished for more as he licked the cloth clean. He left the old globelight beside the stream and pulled the last one from his pack. As expected, it wasn't very bright, but it was something. This was his last chance to make it to daylight assuming this cave even led to daylight. The thought had occurred to him from the beginning, but he shoved it aside. There had to be daylight. But it was just one turn after another along the river bed and he could sense the darkness circling him, waiting to pounce. Finally, the light was nothing but a dim glow in his hand. Enough to see the globelight itself, but not enough to illuminate the cave. He set it down and continued by feel, moving slowly along the side of the cave and hoping there were no sudden drops. It was grueling to go so slow and he finally collapsed and fell asleep again.

He woke to sound. He listened carefully and heard it again. It sounded like wind in the distance, like the first time he had found his way to the cliff face. He must be close! His instinct was to run, but he had to go slow. To fall and injure himself now when he was so close to the outside would be unbearable. Then very suddenly he noticed that it wasn't as dark. He still couldn't see, but now there were shades of black instead of just solid inky black. The shades of black became dark grey and gradually there was enough light to see the floor and walls. Five minutes later he stood at the mouth of the cave where the remnants of his river tumbled out of the cliff face. It was just a trickle now, but it must have been a spectacular waterfall before he blocked it off.

"YEAHHHHHHHH! I made it! I'm alive! I'm free!"

His voice disappeared into the wind without an echo and he suddenly felt silly for yelling. What now? This was a better place to die than the darkness of the caverns, but he didn't want to die. He could try to climb up or climb down. Up sounded better. He guessed he was halfway up the cliff already so that was a good start.

The last of his food was gone, but water would be the problem. There might not be any more on the cliffs once he started climbing. He drank as much as he could from the remaining stream, then started up the route on the left side of the cave. It didn't look promising, but Kraster had climbed enough to know that the best looking routes could end abruptly and the least promising could sometimes take you the furthest. He just focused on the climb. The route split several times and he had to backtrack over and over, but it was two steps forward, one step back. So far, so good, but he realized daylight would be a bigger problem than water. In retrospect, he should have waited until the next morning to start the climb, just to give himself a full day. He'd never climbed at night nor had he ever slept on the cliffs. It was becoming clear he would have to do one or the other. The sun finally dropped below the distant desert sands and dusk gently became twilight. The climbing route was good but there was nowhere to stop and rest; certainly nowhere to fall asleep.

He was moving horizontally along the route when it ended. This was the worst thing he could imagine. There was a place for one foot and his last handholds, then the rock was smooth in every direction. It was almost dark but he thought he could see a ledge down and to his right. It would require jumping as far as he could and then a slide down the cliff face before he could attempt to grab it. If he missed, the next stop would likely be his last. And worse, he wasn't even sure it was a ledge. In this light, it might be a shadow, or a dark colored patch of rock. What were his options? He could try to stay at this spot until morning so he could see the ledge better, but he didn't think he'd be able to hold on that long. He could try to go back down, but there hadn't been a place to stop and rest in a long time. Besides, he would be trying to go down in near-darkness. Was there another option? He wracked his brain trying to find a better choice. Every moment he waited it got darker.

The skeletons at the bottom of the crack in the cliff face came back to him now. Maybe they had been forced to make similarly crazy decisions. No more time to wonder. He jumped as far as he could, then slid down the cliff, trying to slow himself with his hands and feet. It didn't help and he accelerated quickly. His feet hit the ledge and sent shockwaves up his spine, then they slipped off and he grabbed at it desperately with his hands. He had it! He hung from the ledge and tried to find a foothold but there was nothing. Hanging from the ledge with his hands, he started moving hand over hand to his right along the ledge. It was easy to grip and it continued to run slightly upward, but it was getting steadily narrower. Darkness had settled in; everything was by feel. There were still no footholds and his hands were hurting. He could tell they were bleeding; he probably sliced them on the ledge when he first grabbed it going so fast. They hadn't hurt at first, but now they were throbbing. The ledge became a crack that finally became too thin for his fingers to fit. This was it. His only remaining option was to let go and hope there was something else to grab onto below him. He couldn't see anything but he knew his fingers were about to give out anyway.

He let go, slid down the cliff and slammed into the top of an outcropping. It was far enough the landing hurt, but not far enough that it broke his legs. His fingers instinctively found edges and he held on, waiting for his breathing and heart rate to slow. The outcropping wasn't huge but it was big enough. He maneuvered to his left and wedged himself between two rocks so he wouldn't fall if he fell asleep. Maybe someone would find his skeleton right there in a few hundred years. But no, that wouldn't happen. He was alive. Injured, but not severely. He would wait until daybreak and try again.

CHAPTER TWENTY NINE

GENTLE

Myree couldn't sleep. She'd been having trouble ever since she came down from the mesa, but it was even worse now; especially in the resistance cave. It felt like a trap down there. At least out here in the forest she could make a run for it if King Marik's guards found them. It was cool but she was under a small pile of blankets. The stars were an unexpected bonus. She had always liked the stars, but now she was starting to know them. She would pull out the Sun pendant and feel the stone in the darkness while trying to imagine another world hidden in the sky. It was distracting, and usually it was enough for her to fall asleep.

Ena struggled to fall asleep too. Her injuries from the rescue attempt were all surface level and she was healing quickly. Myree listened for hints that Ena was awake, but she didn't want to wake her if she was dozing off.

"Hey, Myree, are you awake?"

"Yeah, I was just wondering if you were awake!"

"I thought I could hear you moving. Can I ask you a question?"

"Of course."

"I can tell something's bothering you. At first I thought it was part of the way you grieve, but there's something else to it. You seem annoyed when people talk to you about Kraster. Something's wrong. What is it? Aren't you proud of him?"

"Yeah, I'm proud of him. It's just that recently… I can't say it. It seems so petty, especially now that he's gone. And I'm annoyed you can tell I'm annoyed!"

"Myree. Tell me."

"I can't. You'll think I'm a horrible person if I tell you."

"You have to tell someone. I promise not to tell anyone."

It took Myree a few seconds to decide how to say it. "I don't just want to be Kraster's sister. That's it in a nutshell. I mean, I want to be more than just Kraster's sister."

Ena laughed softly. "You're not a horrible person."

"I don't know. How can I be so self-centered, especially now that he's gone. I loved having him as my brother, don't get me wrong, but the only thing anyone cares about is that I'm Kraster's sister. Everyone comes up to me and talks about how great it is to meet Kraster's sister. Now that he's dead, and especially because he died a hero, I don't think I'll ever get a chance to be anything but his sister. See? You can't think of anything to say. You know I'm right."

"You might be right - I'm not sure. Maybe with some time others will start to see you for who you are."

"Come on. Even you, when we first met, you said something about me being Kraster's sister. That was just because he made the jump too young."

"I don't remember but I don't doubt it. But Myree, I tried to save Cindl because I thought it would be important to you, not because she was important to Kraster. So maybe I'm the perfect example. Maybe I started out thinking of you as Kraster's sister, but now I think of you as my best friend."

Ena's words froze her thought process; forcing her to adjust. "Thank you again for doing that. I still can't believe you tried it! My crazy best friend. I'm sorry. I'm a jerk for using you as an example."

"You're not a jerk. I'm sorry I didn't notice before. Kraster leaves a big shadow, and it's even bigger now than when we decided to come down."

"You know, I've been living in his shadow since I was eight, but it never bothered me until we came down. I wonder why."

"Maybe it's just part of getting older."

"Yeah maybe. I really idolized him as a kid. Probably even more than I would have if he hadn't jumped. So really, I liked being known as Kraster's sister for most of my life. But then, well, I haven't exactly grown up completely, but I'm a lot older now. You know what it is?" Myree groaned. "I'm too embarrassed to say it."

"Okay. What else should we talk about?"

"Ena! Fine I'll tell you. I thought making that jump and heading off to find Kraster would be worth some respect. Just for me. You know - brave Myree. But even after all of our adventure, I'm still just Kraster's sister. That sounds so selfish. Everyone look at me! I'm important too!"

"Sounds like a pretty normal reaction to me. I'm not sure exactly how you're supposed to feel or act in this situation. I imagine I would crave the same thing."

"Oh, that's a really good word for it. Crave. It makes me think I need to face it, really identify it for what it is, and fight it."

"Is it wrong? To want to be your own person? Do you need to fight it?'

"Well, I can think of a lot of 'normal' impulses that are still worth fighting. But when you say it like that it sounds fine doesn't it? I'm reacting to something. I got it. It might be perfectly natural to want to be my own person, but I think it's wrong to be making decisions just to selfishly build my own reputation. No, that's not quite it." Myree rolled onto her side and propped up her head with her hand.

"How about this. It's wrong to be obsessed with what others think of you."

"Not bad, Ena. The craving for attention is normal, but maybe giving in to it is wrong?"

"Do you really want to be famous? Or important anyway?"

"Oh sure. I want to be famous without having to talk in front of anyone." She said it as a joke but wondered if it might be true. "Seriously though, it seems like it's always the guys that get the glory. Don't you think? People like Kraster. Sometimes I think I should try to be more like him, but I'm not. I'm quieter. Gentler."

"Gentler! Like when you attacked the larren holding the globelight! I'll never forget that as long as I live. I mean, it was terrifying, but now that I can look back on it from a safe distance, it's pretty funny. What were you thinking?"

They both laughed quietly. "I can hardly believe it either! I'm pretty sure I just didn't have time to think about it or I never would have done it. You know me, that was the exception, not the rule. That's not who I really am."

"It's a part of who you are."

"You know what I mean. Maybe that was the emergency

me, not the normal me. I just wonder if there's any glory out there for a quiet, gentle girl like me."

"Myree, those of us who've really gotten to know you, and I think I'm near the top of that list, well, we know you're an incredible person. I have no idea if you'll ever get the same attention and glory that some people get, but I don't care. You're quiet and sometimes gentle; I'll grant you that. You're also the person who didn't abandon me even when that decision might've killed you. You might be quiet, but you're the most determined individual I've ever met - human or larren! I've never wanted to tell you this because you might get mad, but I'm glad we never made it to the slave camp when Kraster was alive. You would have tried charging past the guards or something. I don't think I could have talked you out of it. And maybe it's not the normal you, but the emergency Myree is pretty awesome!" She was sitting up now but wasn't done. "Now that I've said all that, what I really want to say is, if a girl like you doesn't get any glory, then the problem's with the world, not with you. So don't change too much on me."

"I don't know what to say. Thanks Ena."

"You're welcome."

"You know, this might sound strange after all the questions I still have, but I'm starting to finally understand who I am - a little anyway. It's the best thing to come out of this whole disaster."

"What do you think of her; this Myree person?"

"I like her." Myree's voice betrayed the smile that had spread across her face in the darkness.

CHAPTER THIRTY

ASHAMED

CINDL AND MYREE rested after climbing for two hours. The resistance helped them get to the beginning of the old climbing route, and now the forest stretched out below them. Myree glanced down but then forced her gaze back up toward the horizon. The parting with Ena was too fresh. She was scared she would see her down among the trees watching them climb away. Going back to her parents was the right thing to do - she was sure of it - but that didn't make the parting with Ena any easier.

"How're you doing, Myree?"

"Good. Ready for a break, but it's not as hard as I thought it would be. I think we're making good time."

"I agree. I keep waiting for it to get harder." Cindl studied Myree to make sure she wasn't playing dumb. "I meant the other kind of 'how are you doing.'"

"Oh. Okay, I guess. I'm scared to look down in case Ena's still there watching us."

"I don't see her. We're high enough that even if you could make out a larren you wouldn't be able to tell if it was Ena."

Myree allowed herself to look down at the trees and meadow. Cindl was right, it would be hard to know if a larren below was Ena. Still, she would assume any larren was Ena right now. She looked back toward the distant desert.

"She was my best friend."

"I can see why. I've never met a better larren. She'll be okay. The resistance will take care of her."

"Yeah, I know she'll be okay, but I'm still really going to miss her. When I'm not thinking about that, I'm trying to decide how to tell my parents that Kraster's dead. Are they better off not knowing?"

"No, I'd want to know. It'll be hard on them though. They'll need to process their grief over Kraster and their happiness to have you back at the same time. I'm not sure how you do that."

"I think they'll be mad at me too, so add that to the mix of emotions."

"Yeah, maybe, but I think that will take a very distant third place."

"What are we going to tell everyone up there?"

"I've been thinking about that too. My guess is that the humans and larrens have separated themselves even more after you and Ena jumped. From what you've told me, the larrens are probably starting to get really desperate. For all we know, war could have broken out on the mesa already. And if they aren't at war now, we might trigger a war when we tell them what we know."

"I wish this route ended somewhere else on the mesa. We'll be greeted by larrens, not humans."

"Me too. Do you think we could sneak out of the Crimson

Room without anyone seeing us? How well do you remember it?"

"I remember the Crimson room itself really well, but the passageways to get there are another story. The whole place was pretty empty when I visited. We could try, but if they find us sneaking around their temple, we'll look really guilty. I think we should announce ourselves as soon as we get there."

"They're going to want to know how much we know about the Cliff War and about how humans were treated."

"Wait, you think Jesh knows about the Cliff War?"

"I do. I don't think all the mesa larrens know about it, but Jesh does. I'll bet he doesn't tell everyone about the climbing route because he would have to tell everyone about the Cliff War too. What I don't understand is how they kept it a secret for so long."

"I'm sure you're right now that I think about it. Jesh told me there were parts of the story he couldn't tell me. I didn't push him on it. He's friendly, but you just sort of understand that he's in charge. And I wanted to get out of there and go find Kraster."

Cindl was looking more serious now. "Here's the thing; if Jesh knows about what the larrens did but has kept it a secret, he probably won't want us telling the humans what we've learned. I think we need to keep it all to ourselves until we get back among humans."

"What should we say then?"

"How about, we tell him the larrens are in bad shape down on the base. On our way to the climbing route we stopped at the ruins of an old city call Rreker. There were still a handful of larrens living there, and you could tell it had once been a magnificent city. None of the larrens we talked to knew anything about a route up the cliffs. You still have the Sun Pendant so we can just say you never needed it."

"If he asks us more detailed questions, we should just say we don't know."

"Okay, let's try it and focus on getting to humans as soon as possible."

The climb went smoothly. It took two and a half days of climbing. The top half was a lot harder than the bottom, but there were only a few places that were really difficult. It was mid-day when they clambered up the last stretch and found themselves facing a dumbfounded guard in the Crimson Room. There had been guards posted there for hundreds of years and this was the first time they were actually needed. They were separated into two rooms so Jesh could speak to each of them alone. Myree was getting increasingly nervous as she waited for her turn and wondered if the long wait was designed to rattle her. She had to admit it was working.

Jesh walked in and greeted Myree with disarming warmth. "Myree! I can't tell you how happy I am to see you again! I hoped you would find the route and return, but I didn't know if you'd make it."

"Great to see you too Jesh. I'm anxious to see my parents although I'm sure Cindl told you that I have to give them bad news about Kraster."

"She did. I'm terribly sorry to hear that. I hoped you would find him. Look, before you say anything else, there is something I need to tell you. As you mentioned, I just talked to Cindl. She mentioned that Rreker was almost deserted, but I know that isn't the case. On clear nights, we can see the lights of Rreker from our side of the mesa. In fact, that's the main reason we haven't allowed humans to our edge of the cliffs.

Once a year, they have a huge festival as they have been doing for a thousand years. The city is lit up and they build a large fire that is easy to see even on hazy evenings. So I know Cindl has decided to lie to me. I didn't tell her that I know this, so I don't know why she is lying, but I have some guesses. I just wanted to tell you that before we started. You can lie to me as well if you wish, but I'm not going to lie to you."

"We were scared you wouldn't let us leave if we told you everything we learned."

Jesh looked at Myree carefully. He looked sad but not angry. "If I've given you a reason to think I would do that, I apologize. I wanted a chance to talk to you first, but you will be free to go home in a few minutes. Did you learn about the Old War when you were down in the forest?"

"The Cliff War?"

"I suppose they would have a different name for it. You probably know more about it than I do."

"We guessed that you must know about it from the kids who climbed the cliff five hundred years ago."

This seemed to deflate Jesh completely and he sank into the chair next to Myree. "You know about the children." He was talking to himself more than Myree.

"Why haven't you told the humans any of this?"

Jesh sat up straighter in his seat and smiled at Myree. "I'm supposed to be asking you questions. No, no, don't apologize. You have instantly cut to the heart of the issue again. It is because we, the larrens who know, are ashamed of that history and have kept it a secret."

"How could you keep something this important a secret for so long?"

"Myree, it's time to reveal all of this. But I would like to tell it to everyone if you don't mind. I'm going to escort you and Cindl to human territory now. Please tell them that I have a story to tell everyone. Let's gather all the humans and larrens at Speaker's Rock tomorrow morning, two hours after the sun rises. I will explain everything. You should know that my story will be explosive and could trigger a war between us."

"We thought there might already be a war going on."

"No, not yet. The larrens are getting restless and our food stores are getting dangerously low. Part of my willingness to risk a war by telling our history is that I now believe war will erupt on its own very soon anyway. I will give you a small hint. It would not be the first war between larrens and humans on the mesa."

Jesh rose and offered to help Myree up.

"Oh, I almost forgot, here's the pendant back. I never had a chance to show it to the king."

"I'd like you to keep it. You deserve it more than I do."

CHAPTER THIRTY ONE

SCARS AND SMILES

KRASTER WAS WEAK. He hadn't found any water on his climb, his body was battered, and the cuts on his hands were infected. His fever was worse and it was getting harder to concentrate. For what felt like the thousandth time, he was at a dead end. This time he was so close to the top it was infuriating. He backtracked to a small cave he'd passed earlier and crawled inward hoping for a passage higher. Just as he was about to give up, he noticed that the roof of the cave was partially made of dirt. It felt like there were small roots hanging out of the roof! He started digging frantically upward. He pulled down large rocks and pushed them behind him, blocking his retreat in the process. The pain in his hands was terrible but the digging itself was getting easier; more dirt and less rock. When his hand finally broke through, his ears popped as the wind on the mesa pulled air out of the cave. As soon as the hole was big enough, he squeezed up onto the mesa and rolled onto his back in the grass. His body twitched from the exertion without the fuel to sustain it, but somehow, he had made it! The cool mesa breeze was familiar and sliced through what remained of his clothes.

He had to move; had to find food and water. He had to find his Mom and Dad and Myree. He had to tell everyone what was happening down in the forests. But he couldn't move. There was nothing left, no more reserves to pull from. Even his breathing was hard.

"Help! Help! I need help!"

The effort of yelling pushed him over the edge. He could feel his mind slipping toward unconsciousness, but not before he heard someone yell back. Something about 'who is it?' and 'we're coming." He lost consciousness knowing he'd been found.

He woke up, or was woken up, and told he had to drink something. The voice was stern and he didn't have the will or desire to resist. They made him swallow something then take another drink. The voice was familiar but he couldn't place it and he slipped back to sleep.

Again, they woke him and repeated the steps, urging him to drink a little more this time, and try to take two bites. The third time they woke him, he could stay awake longer as he ate and drank. His Mom and Dad were beside him telling him not to speak, just to eat, drink and rest. Myree was on the other side holding his hand with tears and a smile. She looked so much older! Cindl stood behind Myree looking concerned but trying to smile. He tried to say something, but couldn't. They told him to go back to sleep and he did.

When he woke up again, his mind was finally clear and he was hungry. The curtain in his window was open which always let the first rays of the sunrise right onto his pillow. He blinked and looked around at his old room. Everything was as he remembered it. Beside his bed, Myree was sleeping on the floor. He knew it was her at the same moment that he wondered if it could be; she was so different! He'd tried to imagine what she might look like a million times, but now the real version immediately replaced them all. Her face looked so peaceful, but her hands were scratched and scabbed, and there were two large scars on her arm just below her right elbow.

"Myree. Myree! Wake up." Her eyes opened halfway and she blinked to make sense of the world, and then she saw Kraster's face looking over the edge of his bed.

"Kraster!" She jumped up and gave him the best hug of his life. "Oh Kraster! I never thought I'd see you again."

"Me neither. I'm so glad you're here! I've been scared you'd glide down once you turned 16. I never should have left."

"Kraster, I did glide down."

"What? But? What do you mean you glided down?"

"It's a really long story, can I tell you later?"

"You climbed back up?" He looked at her hands again. Myree noticed and held them up for inspection.

"Yes. I suppose that's the short version!" They both laughed as if it were the best joke in the world.

"Myree, I hardly recognize you! I can tell it's you, but it's like you're also a completely different person. Definitely not the little kid I left behind."

"Well, you're not exactly the kid I remember either!"

"Yeah, but you don't seem quite as shocked as I feel."

"I've been helping take care of you for the last two days so I have a bit of an advantage there. Trust me, I felt the same way about you. Actually, I'm not sure any of us would have recognized you with all your scars…", she stopped, wondering if she shouldn't have mentioned them, "but Cindl recognized you immediately, and then once we all looked closer..."

"Cindl's here? How in the world? She must have climbed with you?"

"That's right, but that's part of my long story remember?" She traced one of the scars on Kraster's temple. "She's told us a lot of stories about you over the last several days. I'm sorry you had to go through some of that."

"Me too. I see you have a few yourself." He nodded at her arm.

"Oh, I don't care about those. These are the ones I hate." She turned her head all the way to the right so Kraster could see the scar on the left side of her nose and another on her jawline. They weren't as bad as Kraster's but he instinctively understood her fears. "I can't hide my face."

Kraster held her hand tightly. "I'm sorry Myree. Larrens?"

"Yeah. I may have attacked a larren. How did we go from happy to sad in thirty seconds!"

"You attacked a larren? My little sister?"

"I thought I could take him."

Kraster laughed too hard and his head started throbbing. "Well, that was funny."

"I hear Mom and Dad coming. I guess they heard you laughing. I'll go grab some breakfast for us and be right back."

"Myree, wait. Did you glide down to find me?"

"Who else?"

"Thank you. I wish you hadn't, but it means a lot that you did. I think those scars are my fault."

"They're not your fault! Hey, I thought you were dead three days ago. I'm lucky to be alive myself. That's what I'm going to focus on. I love you, brother."

"I love you too, Myree. I'm glad you're safe." She gave him a soft slow-punch on the cheek, then hurried off to the kitchen to grab some food just as her mom entered the room.

"Kraster! My boy! I thought I'd lost you forever. Are you feeling any better?"

"Mom! Mom, I'm so sorry. I never should have…"

"Shhh. Never mind all that. All I care about right now is that you're awake and alive. You're fever was so high. I thought I might lose you again." She sat beside him holding his hand and kissing his forehead.

"Dad!"

"Son! It's so good to hear your voice!"

The next two hours were the happiest of their lives. They made Kraster eat and drink while they took turns answering his barrage of questions. Every story was incredible, every joke hilarious, and every tear and smile from the bottom of their hearts.

CHAPTER THIRTY TWO

DECISIONS

THE SUN WAS an hour old in the morning sky. Myree and Kraster sat together at the cliffs - happy to be together and nervous about the future. Kraster had missed the first meeting when Jesh explained how larrens and humans had been trapped on the mesa by an earthquake. Then Cindl recounted the history of the Cliff War and explained the situation between humans and larrens down below. Jesh finished with an account of what happened on the mesa after the human children arrived with messages about the war below. Humans and most larrens heard their full history for the first time.

A little over five hundred years earlier, a young girl appeared at the top of the cliffs with a message from the larren king stamped onto a small copper plate she was wearing on a leather strap around her neck. The message told of a war with the humans and asked for help. Since every larren was as strong as two or three humans, every pair that glided down would tip the war in the larren's favor. The next day, another girl appeared at the same spot, then a gradual trickle of children continued to arrive. Each had their own story of war, but were pushed to climb by the promise that if they made it, their families would be spared. The larrens tried to keep the war a secret, but the news spread from larren to larren and finally to the humans as well. They had been living happily together, but the knowledge of a war between them below and the fact that the larrens would capture children and force them to climb the cliffs created a rift between them. There were pleas for peace, for patience, for calm heads, but the violence eventually broke and quickly swept across the mesa. The larrens were stronger, and in the passion of war, they killed every human on the mesa. It was only after this atrocity that they realized their mistake. They would not be able to glide down to the forests without humans. Fortunately for them, the train of children continued to appear at the spot where the larrens now had their Crimson Room.

If the first atrocity could be blamed on passion and war, the second atrocity was premeditated and deliberate. The children arriving on the cliffs were kept in camps and treated with kindness; but they were prisoners. As these children grew up and started having children of their own, those children were taken and raised by the larrens, never knowing that their human parents were a few kilometers away. Eventually, the prisoners stopped having more children. They understood that the babies would be taken from them and their defiance eventually trumped all other passions. Meanwhile the stream of new children coming up the cliffs ended because the war below was over. The humans had made a mistake, extended themselves too far and were crushed. They were all either killed or fled into the desert hoping to find the fabled Jadin Mountains.

Years later, when some of the larren-raised children were

old enough, one was sent down with a message for the larren king below - never send anyone up the cliffs again unless the mesa larrens send down a girl with sun around her neck. The Sun Pendant was older than their collective written history and had been famous long before the Finger collapsed. The rule to never ask a human younger than sixteen to make the jump was a silent apology for the way human children were treated. Finally, the larrens held a meeting and decided not to tell the next generation about what happened. Only members of the Larren Council would retain the truth.

The walls going up changed everything. As the larrens' predicament became desperate, Jesh received news that Kraster's sister was outside the walls and had formed a friendship with a young larren. He gave her the sun pendant expecting her to go looking for Kraster. He hoped the larrens below would understand the significance 500 years later, and if they allowed some humans to climb the cliffs, then everyone on the mesa would know that it wasn't a one-way trip. He would still have to explain their past, but he could do it at the same time that he offered them the hope of reunions. In short, he was trying to avoid another war. He asked everyone to go home to think and meet back in a week. "Somehow", he had said, "we all have to confront the horror of our past and decide how to live together in the future".

Myree leaned against Kraster and let her head rest on his shoulder. As different as he looked, when he smiled and talked, he was so familiar. Older, more intense, but still Kraster.

"What are you going to say at the meeting?"

"Me?"

"Yes you! Everyone will want to know what you think. You're a larger-than-life legend down below, and, you're kind of a living legend up here too. The boy who crushed a 500-year-old larren project and the first boy to find his own way up the cliffs." She used her best announcer voice for the last bit.

"You're as much of a legend as I am. I love the globe-light story."

"I'm a little glad you think so, but I know I'm not. Everyone admires your decisions; I hear people talk about it. No one thinks I was brilliant for going after you."

"Every big decision I've made has been a disaster. Seriously, I don't understand why people don't see that."

"I think it's the way you make decisions. You're always trying to do the right thing even when it costs you."

"Well I try, but at some point my track record should matter, shouldn't it?"

"Except, most of us really don't know what to do. I know I'm hoping you have an idea."

"Myree, you're my sister. I seriously doubt most people feel that way."

"Only one way to find out. The meeting's in a couple hours. You want to practice your speech on me?"

"No! I haven't decided yet if I'm going to say anything."

"But you have something to say, don't you?"

"I guess. I mean, yes, I do. I've been working on an idea for the last three days, but I'm hoping someone else will have a better one. What do you think we should do?"

"I told you, I don't know. I wasn't kidding. Besides, I always have ulterior motives. I want to be famous, or have people like me. Stupid stuff like that. Even when I went after you, I imagined how brave I'd seem to everyone."

Kraster glanced at his sister with a new level of admiration. "You can't let that stop you. If we only did the right thing when our motivations were perfect, we'd never do anything good. Besides, everyone but you gave up on me. I'll never forget that, Myree."

It was a good place for silence and they sat together thinking for a long time.

"What was it like working on the tunnel? I mean, I've heard a lot of what happened, but, what was it like? I'm not asking this very well. I keep trying to imagine how I would think and feel if it had been me."

"It changed. At the beginning it was a mix of scary and wonderful. I was so glad to be back with humans, but everything was new and they were making me climb into caves alone." He smiled at the memory. "It seems funny to me now, but I was so scared going into those caves alone the first few times. And then I started to get used to it. There was a stretch in the middle when I was really happy. Cindl told you the Rain Games story; that will probably be one of my best memories for the rest of my life. But after the beating, I started to change for the worse. I already hated the larrens; that started almost as soon as Cindl and I were captured, but it got so much worse. And I started to give up. I hope I never feel that way again. I used to think of you and Mom and Dad all the time. Mostly I worried that you'd come looking for me as soon as you were old enough. If I'd known about the walls I probably wouldn't have worried so much, although obviously they didn't stop you. So when I saw a chance to strike a blow, even at the cost of my life, I was willing to take it. It doesn't seem quite as noble after hearing all that does it? And you know the worst part? I think even that decision might have been a mistake."

"Really?"

"Yeah. I mean, if we had a tunnel, the larrens below could

come up to the mesa in the winter to deposit their pods like they used to. Then they wouldn't be threatened by the growing human population. When the larren population up here got too large and their food supply got low, some of them could just walk down to the forest. No need to recruit or trick humans to take them down."

"Ena told me a lot of larrens in the resistance felt that way, but right now larrens need us. It's our only real bargaining chip. If there was a tunnel, what would prevent them from just killing us all?"

"Nothing I guess. But Ena would never kill you. There are some really good larrens and some really bad ones; just like with humans. I would love for the good ones to have a turn in charge. The bad ones have had too much influence for too long. Maybe we can build a relationship that isn't based on bargaining chips."

"They said my friendship with Ena was sending ripples through the whole larren population down below. I'm still not entirely sure why it would, but they said it was important."

"Cindl told me about that. She kept trying to convince me in the camp that some of the larrens were compassionate; the way some of them looked at us or little things they would say. I could never let myself see it at the time. I'm glad you got to know her. She held on to her goodness through everything. I was losing mine. I'm almost sure I would have lost it without her."

"I like her. I think Mom's jealous."

"Yeah, I'll bet she is. We've both treated Mom horribly you know."

"I know."

"And I know she'll hate what I'm thinking."

"What are you going to do?"

"I have an idea, but..."

"But...?"

"I seem to make bad decisions, remember? Even if I could get everyone to listen, I'm not sure I should try."

"Kraster, everyone looks up to you. We know you might be wrong; or that things could turn out poorly. In fact, I'll bet a lot of people will have a grand time criticizing you when this is all over - it makes us feel important without having to make the decision ourselves. But, I'm almost positive people want to know what you think. If you want to lead a group of us back down, there will be a crowd ready to follow."

Kraster couldn't hide his shock. "Are you guessing or did you hear about my plan?"

"Looks like I guessed right! It just seemed like the most likely thing you'd do. You're right though; Mom will hate it."

"I hope Mom hasn't figured it out too." Kraster scuffed up her hair in retaliation. She tried to get him back but he fought her off. "I always thought you'd end up being smarter than me, but I wasn't expecting it to happen so soon."

Myree looked to see if he was joking, but he seemed serious. She couldn't think of anything to say, but she felt taller somehow.

CHAPTER THIRTY THREE
SPEAKER'S ROCK

SPEAKER'S ROCK WAS literally a rock that stuck out of the water. It was at a spot where the river spread out into a large pool. Normally, it was just the most popular spot to swim, but it also served as a natural amphitheater for large gatherings. The water was still chilly in early June, so you really had to want to speak to swim out to the rock. Humans and larrens crowded in on their respective sides of the pool and for two hours a steady stream of them swam out to give their opinion. 'We should stop sending anyone down to the forest'. 'We should just avoid each other on the mesa because there's no way to trust each other anymore'. 'We should forgive each other and live together in peace'. 'We should just get this over with and fight each other now'. Finally, the last speaker finished and swam back to the larren side. A silence folded around the crowd like an itchy blanket.

Myree sat with her family on the human side about ten people back from the edge of the water. She'd expected her Dad to swim out and say something, but he remained seated on her left. Kraster looked nervous on her right. He kept shifting in his spot but hadn't made a move to stand.

"Is there anyone else who would like to speak?" There was an edge of panic in Jesh's voice. This had not gone well. There was no emerging consensus and the tension was obviously higher than he expected. The crowd was agitated; she could feel it and sometimes hear it.

She leaned over so she could whisper. "Kraster, if you don't say something now, Jesh is going to dismiss everyone. Did anyone say what you were going to say?"

"No." But he looked sick and he stayed in his spot.

"Kraster. Go."

Kraster looked up and nodded. He reminded her of their mom after she'd been arguing with their dad for too long. Tired and drained and ready to crash, but he stood and glanced around. A rustling spread through the crowd as everyone stared at him or was nudged so they could.

"You don't have to say anything, but would you swim out with me? I'd like you with me for this."

Myree was caught off guard but couldn't say no. "Sure, I'll go with you."

People leaned out of the way to let them move down to the water. Kraster immediately dove in and started swimming. Myree would have preferred to ease in but she tightened her muscles, hardened her mind and dove in after him. She'd never done that before and the shock of it almost made her inhale the cool water. Everything faded except getting to Speaker's Rock as fast as possible. As she took the last few strokes, Kraster was holding out his hand and pulled her out of the water.

"Sorry, I didn't think it would be so cold. You mad?"

"A little! Wow. I have to swim back when you're done so I'll probably be really mad later."

Kraster smiled. She was tense and distracted, but the swim had the opposite effect on Kraster. He looked ready. The crowd must have heard them because she could see a lot of smiles and felt her cheeks flush. Kraster dried himself off quickly and stepped to the edge of the rock. Myree sat down next to Jesh and he handed her one of the few remaining towels.

"Hi everyone. My name's Kraster." He grinned, realizing how silly that sounded but recovered quickly. "I guess most of you know my story. I need to start with a confession. Until a week ago, I blamed all larrens for the cruelty of some larrens. Starting with Wilton, almost every larren I met was trying to trick me or hurt me. Maybe kill me. When I learned what larrens did in the past, sending all those kids up the cliffs, it just confirmed everything I already believed. I hated larrens. I know that's not fair, but it's true. I'm sure I'm not the only human to think that way.

"But when I got back up here, I heard about Ena. I couldn't hate her. I'm convinced my sister would be dead if Ena hadn't risked everything to stay with her, to fight alongside her. Ena isn't my enemy, she's the opposite. I hope she's safe and happy down below. If I could, I'd try to protect her and take care of her. And then, hearing about Ena reminded me of Mennow. Where are you Mennow? There you are. I remember telling my mom you were my best friend. We used to play king of the rock - right here! I had the chance to reconnect with Mennow a few days ago and he's still awesome. I don't hate Mennow either. Oh, and I forgot to mention - Ena risked her life again to save Cindl. Two people who matter a lot to me are alive because of a larren. I hope I get to meet her someday.

"But even more important, there's a larren resistance down below. Thousands of them. Maybe you could convince me that Ena's an exception, or that my childhood friendship with Mennow isn't relevant. That's possible. But I can't ignore thousands of larrens who are organized to end human slavery. If Ena's actions speak to my emotions, the resistance speaks to my reason.

"So I owe all of you larrens an apology. I hope you can forgive me for hating you unjustly. And be patient with me as I try to change how I think and speak. I'm sure I'll slip up sometime but remind me of what I just said and I'll keep trying to change.

"That gets me to a point I'm still wrestling with, but I think it's important. How should we think about each other - humans and larrens? Are we friends or enemies? Are we part of the same group? That's the big question. At one level there's no one exactly like me. So at one extreme, I'm alone - not part of a group at all. I look out for my own interests more often than I should. But moving up a level is my family. I care about my family and look out for them. I'm willing to give them the benefit of the doubt, and would sacrifice a lot for them. What about the other extreme; the largest group that I care about. Is it humans? If so, then I think we're stuck. But are we also part of a larger group together; humans and larrens? As different as we look, we have so much in common. It's more than just sharing this island in the desert. We have so many of the same thoughts and emotions. Both humans and larrens are smart and creative and daring. So are there any fixed rules or laws of nature that determine whether we see ourselves as us or them? Not that I can come up with. My big realization this week is that we get to choose. We get to choose whether we care for each other or not.

"I can't speak for anyone else, but I've decided that at that first and largest level, I'm going to think of humans and larrens as one group. A larren is not my enemy by being a larren any more than a human is my enemy by being a human.

"That was important for me to work through. It's the new framework for how I think. But it doesn't change the reality that as we gather here right now, larrens down on the base are keeping humans as slaves - treating them as property - with all the callous cruelty that comes with that framework. We used to be ignorant, so we could have all agreed to think of each other as one group and everything probably would have been fine. But we can't un-know what we've learned. As long as human slavery exists below, that knowledge will linger in larren minds. 'Should humans be our equals?' 'Other larrens don't treat them that way.' And humans will have a hidden fear and anger toward larrens. 'What if they decide to enslave us after all?' 'How can I trust this seemingly good larren when I know what other larrens are doing to other humans?' The existence of slavery is a wedge between us. Actually, I think even the memory of slavery will be a wedge between us, but we can't deal with that until we get rid of it in the first place. Everyone who spoke today focused on how we should treat each other on the mesa. Embedded in those comments was the assumption that we can't do anything about what's happening below us. I strongly disagree.

Kraster glanced back at Myree and she noticed some of the tension creeping back into his face. She stood and took a few steps to stand beside him.

"So here's my proposal. If enough of you will join me,

I'm going back down to overthrow King Marik and set the humans free."

There was silence for a couple of seconds and then a few shouts of approval built into a roar that pressed them from both sides. Kraster held up his hand and the crowd quieted.

"If you want to make the jump and are young enough and small enough, find a pair and be at the ledge tomorrow at three in the afternoon. The plan is to send down our army in the largest jump in history, rally the humans and any sympathetic larrens, then march on Rreker. After all of you have jumped, I'll wait until dark and jump off on the other side. I'll try to find the larren resistance and spring the human slaves from the tunnel camp before King Marik even knows we're coming. As a combined force, we'll all attack Rreker eight days from today. You should be able to march around the mesa by then."

"How in the world are you going to jump at night? And why? It's crazy." The voice was from the larren side but Myree couldn't see who it was.

"I'm glad you asked, because I'll need a larren to make the jump with me and, as you're suggesting, it will be dangerous. That's why I can't ask anyone else to do it. I said I would jump at night, but technically I'm going to jump at the first trace of daylight so I have just enough light to make out the cliff face, but hopefully not enough light for anyone to spot us gliding down - assuming anyone's awake to see us. My best chance of finding the resistance is to get down there unseen. Myree and Cindl told me there's a long open meadow stretching along the cliffs near the beginning of the climbing route so I'm planning to circle straight down from the Crimson Room and land in that meadow. As for why - I want to try to free some of the human slaves before King Marik finds out there's an army marching toward him. Once he hears about our army, he might lock up every human to keep them out of the fight. But what I really fear is that he might just decide to kill them. I know this is war and some of us will die, but I want to give them a chance. They were my friends. And even if they weren't, I think it would be worth the risk to try to save them. As a bonus, if I succeed, trust me, they're a tough bunch and will be a real asset in the war. The larren resistance will almost certainly join you on your march, but I'll try to find them first so they can help me free the slaves. Does that make sense?"

There were a lot of nodding heads and verbal approvals.

"Last, Myree is the only one up here who's made the jump without crashing. Cindl and I both survived ours, but that isn't much to brag about. So Myree, I should have asked you ahead of time, but sometime tomorrow, would you give everyone instructions on how to glide down?"

"Sure. I'll plan to be at the ledge all day tomorrow to go over it with anyone that's interested."

"You should all be interested!" The crowd laughed. "Okay, you're dismissed. And see you tomorrow."

The hum of talking instantly filled the air and Kraster turned toward Myree and Jesh. Jesh was standing now too. It was hard to read his face, but he didn't look happy.

"Kraster, I think I should tell you that you will be viewed as either a hero or a villain depending on whether you win this war. I hope you've thought this through very carefully."

"I've tried. Look, I don't know what your intentions are, but after the way you manipulated my sister, I'm sure you'll understand that I don't trust you. I know you were desperate - I can appreciate that, believe me - but I still can't trust you."

"I was desperate to avoid a war. You are leading us straight into one. I won't pretend I approve."

Kraster looked like he was about to reply, but just nodded instead and turned back to Myree.

"I think we should split up. You swim back to the human side and I'll swim over to the larren side."

"I'm planning to stay here until the water gets a lot warmer."

Kraster grinned and pulled her into a hug. "Thanks for being willing to help. I think it'll make a big difference."

"Happy to help."

Kraster dove into the water and swam to the larren side, and Myree slowly eased herself into the cool water and swam to the human side three minutes later.

CHAPTER THIRTY FOUR
THE MAGNIFICENT JUMP

KEM WONDERED IF her eyes were still red. Probably not. Her friends were so mean sometimes. Her mom said she needed new ones, but she didn't understand how hard that would be. Anyway, she was happier now in her favorite hiding place; five meters up in a tree at the edge of the commons meadow outside Lin. There were enough leaves that she was invisible from the ground, but the branches left a gap allowing her to look out at the meadow and cliffs. It wasn't the most comfortable place to rest, but not bad for a tree. It was a place of peace and quiet. The meadow was full of animals grazing, and even their noises were mostly calming.

Her eye caught a flicker of movement up on the cliffs. At first she couldn't find it when she looked for it, but then she saw it again. It wasn't movement on the cliff, it was a pair gliding down! She leaned forward as if the extra distance would help her see better. It looked like they were coming straight toward her. If they didn't change course they were going to land in the meadow and she had the best spot to watch. Then she saw the second pair behind the first one and in a blink she saw the trail of pairs stretching back up toward the top of the cliffs. She had never heard of anything like this.

She needed to clear the animals out of the meadow. There was still time, but she should hurry. She glanced back up as she was starting to climb down and was horrified to see more pairs, but they were closer. She hadn't been looking at the first pair in the trail. There was no time. Kem scrambled down through the branches. The last branch before the ground was big and stretched out into the meadow. She had imagined balancing out and jumping so many times that now she just did it. Her adrenaline pumped through her body as she took the last few steps and jumped off. She landed on her feet and did a forward roll ending up back on her feet. She wished someone could have seen that. Just as she was about to sprint into the meadow she stopped and frantically looked for some sticks. It didn't take long to find some and then she was off running straight down the middle of the meadow screaming and pounding the sticks together to scare the animals. It was working! She was clearing a path down the middle. As she ran she glanced up at the trail of pairs. They were so close. She didn't know if she could run faster, but she tried. Screaming at the animals while she ran was starting to take its toll. It was hard to breathe but she ran and screamed anyway. The first pair glided past her a few meters off the ground. The larren was focused ahead on the landing, but the human girl was looking straight at her smiling. She smiled back and waved, then felt a surge of energy and kept running. By the time she got to the other side, ten pairs had already landed. She stood shaking and panting and watched the first group of pairs finish her work, herding the animals even further away from the middle of the meadow.

People from town were starting to show up too and she watched a group of them carry an injured larren off to the side.

Kem lay down on her back and watched pair after pair pass overhead. It was spectacular to watch and she caught herself smiling into the sky. The only pair she'd ever seen was Myree and Ena about six months earlier, on her eleventh birthday of all days. The last pair before that was Kraster and Wilton and she'd only been four years old back then. Somewhere around the two hundredth pair Kem stopped counting. She'd find out later how many there were. Her breathing was approaching normal again and she sat up in the grass.

"Hey, there you are! Are you the kid that ran down the middle like a maniac?"

Kem turned and looked back toward the voice. It was the girl she'd waved at, but she looked like Myree. Her mind tried to put all the pieces together and just jammed instead. She thought Myree was dead, and you can't come down from the mesa twice. "Myree?"

"Yeah! Have we met?" She held out her hand and helped pull Kem up.

"No, I just remember you from last time you came down. How did you…" Her voice trailed off, unsure what question she even wanted to ask.

"There's a climbing route up the cliffs on the other side, but you'll hear all about that soon. What's your name by the way?"

"Kem."

"It's a pleasure to meet you Kem. I had to come find you after that mad dash down the meadow. That was hilarious and awesome at the same time! I have no idea how many crashes you prevented, but it's a lot. Probably saved several lives today."

Kem tried to act like it was no big deal, but she could feel her face giving her away. "Why are there so many pairs?"

"It's an army. We're going to march to Rreker and overthrow a king. And you helped."

CHAPTER THIRTY FIVE

SPARKS AND STARS

THE MARCH TO Rreker had gone smoothly once it started. Myree had assumed that the humans in and around Lin would be excited to join the revolt, but they needed a couple of days to think it through. On the mesa, Jesh had given everyone time to process the new information, and even then it had taken Kraster's speech to harden everyone's resolve around this course of action. But Kraster was on the other side. Myree made an attempt to be his voice, but it wasn't the same. Still, when they started the march two days later, there were three times as many of them as glided down.

About halfway to Rreker they were met by the larren resistance and former tunnel slaves. Kraster must have succeeded, but no one she met had seen him or knew where he was. She couldn't think of a reason why he wouldn't come find her. Then she started overhearing the rumors. Some said Kraster survived the landing but died later that same day. Another said he was alive but badly injured. The common thread to all the variations was that the resistance was trying to hush things up as a form of damage control. No one knew where Ena was either.

She would have been a mess if Bend hadn't found her. It was impossible to be sad around Bend. He was so excited to meet her and introduced her to all the diggers. It took too long to say "former tunnel slaves" so they had quickly adopted the new name; a new identity. It was an interesting compromise, casting aside the slave label, but keeping the reference to what they'd built.

It was dark now on the seventh day since landing and the army had spread out around Rreker while they still had daylight. Most of the diggers had set up outside the north gate, but a smaller group, including Bend and Myree, were camped outside the northeast gate. They had exchanged a few arrows with the guards on the wall during the day, but in general things were calm. Their campfire was set back well out of archer range and the resistance and diggers had been taking turns teaching each other songs. It was hard to imagine war was about to start.

Myree couldn't help being happy herself. Bend hadn't left her side since they met. At first she thought he was just determined to protect his best friend's sister, but now she thought there was more to it. Bend and several other diggers had made comments that they couldn't believe someone as ugly as Kraster could have such a beautiful sister. It took her two days to realize they weren't joking. Well, they were joking about Kraster, but not about her. The scars on her face didn't bother the diggers. Almost all of them had a few scars of their own. It was her own thoughts about Bend that finally changed her mind. His scars were worse than almost everyone. Both Kraster and Cindl agreed that Bend had received the worst of the beating that night by the guard's fire. She didn't think his scars were beautiful exactly, but they made him feel closer, it was a link between them. They both received their scars from cruel larrens. Bend received his alongside her brother.

She loved the way his eyes followed her when she moved, the way he smiled and laughed at even moderately funny jokes, and the way he sang old songs as if they were brand new. When most people looked at her, their eyes darted to her scars and then she could sense them trying not to look again. Bend would look at her scars like he looked at her hair or lips. She was getting used to the way he looked too and liking him more and more. Maybe he could feel the same way. Sometimes she would grieve for him when she wondered what he would look like without the scars, but it was the same grief she felt for herself and it made her like him more.

It wasn't just Bend that made her happy. Someone had told the globelight fight story and within an hour every digger knew it. Something changed after that. She could feel their admiration and respect. They stopped treating her like a favorite guest and she became a member of their family.

Bend sat beside Myree in the loose circle around the fire. He had been singing earlier, but now he leaned back in silence staring at the sky.

"When I was a kid, my dad told me that all sparks from fires are trying to become stars. They shoot up into the air reaching for glory - to be permanent, remembered - to matter somehow. Sometimes you'll see a big spark that you think will make it for sure, but in a matter of seconds it fades out and disappears. Other times it's a small spark that you don't even notice at first, but it keeps going higher and higher. He said it didn't matter how bright the spark was; all that mattered was how hard they tried; and having a little luck. So there you have it! That's why there are so many more little stars than big stars. The biggest brightest sparks don't think they have to try as hard."

"What a great story. I'm guessing he didn't know how big you'd grow up to be or he might have changed it a little." Myree glanced over to see Bend smiling.

"Yeah, you're probably right. I still think of it every time I sit around a fire. Maybe I like it tonight because I feel so small when I think about attacking those walls. Besides, I'll bet my dad was thinking of people like you when he made the story up."

"Now you're just embarrassing me. I wish I could have met your parents."

"Me too. They would have liked you." They watched the sparks try their hardest for several minutes. "You know, I don't talk about this with anyone, but I was thinking about that story the night they beat me and Kraster and Cindl. I knew what was coming and I knew that sometimes slaves died from those beating. I sat watching that fire wondering how hard I would try. Would I give up? The second thing I was thinking about was my name. It's an unusual name for sure. Before my Mom died, she told me that it had been my dad's idea. They knew I was being born into a difficult life and that I would have to face real hardship. My dad wanted to remind me to bend but never break. She said my Dad used to tell me that when I was little but I don't remember it. Those were the two things that got me through that night. I promised myself I would try harder than I'd ever tried before and that I wouldn't break."

Myree tried to swallow down the lump in her throat. She moved closer and reached out to hold his hand for the first time. The diggers around them were just getting the hang of a new resistance song, their voices combining with the sparks and rising into the speckled blackness.

CHAPTER THIRTY SIX

SIGNAL FIRE

IT WAS MIDNIGHT, seven days after Myree led the first wave down. For what felt like the hundredth time in the last month, Cindl marveled at being part of such an important time in history. And not just present, but really part of it. She'd been there the day Kraster ruined a five-hundred-year project. She and Myree were the first people to climb the route up the cliffs in five hundred years! Everyone thought this was Kraster's plan, but they had planned it all out together as he recovered his strength on the mesa. And now, she was hidden inside Rreker on the eve of war.

Almost everyone thought Kraster had glided down, but the plan had always been for her to go. A hundred larrens volunteered to make the jump with Kraster, and Mennow helped narrow the list down to three. Two were backups in case their first choice balked at gliding down with an adult when they found out about the last second switch. But the backups weren't needed. When it was finally time to jump, Cindl thought she was more nervous than the larren. Both times she had jumped with a larren had resulted in a crash. The first, when she was sixteen, was just bad luck. A gust of wind had caught them just before landing and pushed them against a hillside. She had walked away with just scratches, but her pair had broken several bones. Of course, the second time had been the jailbreak. Ena insisted that it hadn't felt much different than gliding with Myree and they decided the tower simply wasn't tall enough to let them clear the trees. Even knowing all that, tying herself to another larren for a third jump required more courage than she'd ever had to muster. But she had to do it. The plan didn't make sense unless she went first.

Everything had gone reasonably well. They glided down in a spiral from the Crimson Room and landed in the meadow near the beginning of the climbing route. The landing had been a little hard, but she attributed that to the low visibility. As planned, they jumped just as the sky was showing the first blues of morning, but it was effectively still dark. They had to rely on Cindl's vision and it had proven difficult to communicate how close they were to the ground. All in all, she wouldn't recommend a night jump to anyone, but they survived and built the three signal fires so Kraster would know they made it.

That already seemed so long ago. She'd been hiding in the forest watching the resistance free the tunnel slaves. Amazing! Now she was part of history again. Rreker was in lockdown, surrounded by an army, but she was inside. The resistance had smuggled almost a hundred diggers into Rreker before King Marik heard about the advancing army. It was a miserable week, crammed into a small hidden nook by herself and hoping the searchers didn't find her. At least that was over. In many ways, everything had been building to this moment - midnight on the seventh day.

She'd asked if Ena could be part of her small team and

the two of them had spent the last half hour enjoying their reunion. It felt good to be with someone she knew. They were both worried about Myree. Keeping her in the dark had been the worst part of this whole plan. Ena thought she would understand, but Cindl wasn't sure.

Ena kept looking at the sky. They were both worried about the same thing.

"Hey, Ena, this will still work. At least it's not raining. Then we'd be in trouble."

"I hope you're right. We should go. I don't see anyone around and it's about time. You ready?"

"I am. Let's go."

Cindl, Ena and two other larrens moved quietly from their hiding place, crossed the street and formed a small pyramid so Cindl could climb up and crawl through a second-floor window. Then the larrens disappeared back into the shadows. It was pitch black inside and she pulled out her globelight. She didn't even shake it, she just needed enough light to find her way around. First she found the stairs and went down to find a door. After making sure she could open it, she locked it again and headed back up to the second floor.

It was one of the oldest buildings that formed the fringe around the center circle of Rreker. No one in their group knew what it was originally built for, but it was currently being used as a warehouse and frankly it probably just needed to be torn down. It was full of items that someone thought might be useful to someone else but that no one ever really wanted again. Everything was covered in thick layers of dust. Using kindling she had brought in her bag, along with anything lying around that looked especially flammable, Cindl started two fires roughly in the middle of the building. She wanted to wait longer and make sure the fires would stay lit, but the smoke was building fast and she knew she had to go. She moved quickly back to the window and signaled for help. As soon as they rebuilt their larren pyramid, Cindl climbed out of the window and back to the ground. The door had only been a back-up plan; they wanted to keep it locked if they could to slow down any attempt to put out the fire. They still hadn't been seen and they watched the building for signs that it was burning inside.

"There! I think I saw a light in the window." They all watched and soon the firelight was flashing out into the night air.

"Nice job Cindl."

"Thanks, Ena." For a moment everything felt like a game. Sneaking around in the dark with your friends hoping the other side didn't see you.

They watched the building for a few more minutes until a section of the roof collapsed and the fire leapt into the sky. The orange flames grew as they watched, forming a giant flashing tower in the heart of Rreker and illuminating the whole center circle with its unsteady light. It was finally getting the attention they hoped for. A large group of Marik's guards were running across the circle from the palace, but it was obvious there was nothing to be done but let the fire burn itself out.

Cindl stepped out into the open in full view of the oncoming guards. She heard the rest of her group step out behind her.

"Down with King Marik! Down with the tyrant!" Cindl yelled at the top of her lungs. Then they were all yelling.

An arrow rattled off a wall a meter to their left; it was time to run. Ena and Cindl followed the two resistance larrens who knew their way around the city. For now, they just needed to lose the guards and after several turns they ducked into another old building and waited in the dark. Their breathing sounded so loud in the silence, but then they heard the bell ringing. Cindl felt a new rush of excitement and a tinge of remorse. A member of the resistance who worked in the palace guard volunteered to ring the bell and the pattern for immediate help rolled across the city. Marik's guards would almost certainly catch him in the next few minutes, but not before he drew troops away from the walls. Between the fire she had lit and the bell, Marik's troops would be in disarray. At least that was the plan.

CHAPTER THIRTY SEVEN
MYREE'S GUARD

IT WAS MIDNIGHT and the campfire was fading. About half the group had gone to bed, and those who remained either sat quietly or chatted in small groups. Myree and Bend were in the same spot, but Bend had fallen asleep ten minutes ago. Myree was tired too but she didn't want to fall asleep yet. Bend's breathing was slow and steady, and she studied his face with a freedom she wouldn't have when he was awake. Anyone who met him and saw that face would be impressed that he could have so much joy after so much suffering. But she knew that underneath that public presentation was a base of sorrow that most people would never see. Kraster had hinted at the same thing up on the mesa and Myree felt it in herself. Bend had allowed her to see both layers. He'd given her special access; it was like receiving a rare gift.

Her thoughts were interrupted by flames shooting into the sky over Rreker's wall. It took a moment to grasp how large the fire must be to look so big from this far away.

"Bend, wake up." She nudged him again and waited for him to sit up. "Look. I think that fire is inside Rreker."

It took him several seconds to focus, then he sat bolt upright. "Wow! That must be huge." Everyone around the campfire had seen it now and was standing up. "We should wake everyone up."

"I agree."

Five minutes later everyone was awake and moving toward the gate. A bell started ringing inside Rreker and froze everyone in their tracks.

"Bend, do you know what's going on?"

"No. I had the impression that there was more to the plan that wasn't being shared, but I don't know what it is."

"You think our side started the fire?"

"Probably. What do you think?"

"I suppose so. I don't know what King Marik would accomplish by lighting it. That means we have people inside Rreker." Even as she said it, the weight of it increased in her mind. If King Marik had to worry about the resistance inside Rreker too, then maybe breaching the walls wasn't as impossible as it looked.

As they approached the wall they received orders not to attack yet. There was obviously a plan in place. This wasn't just going to be a raging mob throwing itself against a massive wall. She checked her quiver to make sure she hadn't dropped any arrows and checked Bend's for him so he wouldn't have to take it off. They were still hidden in the trees but they could see larrens on the wall and hear the commotion inside. She was scared, but not like she had been in the past. This time she felt like the hunter.

They were in the last trees before the open strip of grass outside of the wall. Any further and they would be easy targets. The guards on the wall must have seen movement because she could hear arrows ripping through leaves and hitting wood. She guessed it had been ten minutes since the bell rang when they received word to begin the attack.

Myree notched an arrow as she had been practicing for days, aimed at a guard and let it go. Too short; it hit the wall two meters below the top. She readied her second shot and pulled back further. That was much better. She hadn't been shooting this hard in practice and a kernel of doubt rose in her stomach as she imagined her arrow hitting someone. But that's what this was; it was war. They were shooting at her and she was shooting at them. She let three more arrows fly, each one feeling easier and better.

The attack was stalling, or more accurately, it never managed to build any momentum in the first place. It was loud and tense but both attempts to ram the gate had been driven back and dozens of human and larren fighters lay unmoving. Myree could feel her frustration rising and had a strong urge to make something happen. Maybe run out screaming and firing arrows. She'd never been in a war but she guessed that was how to get killed.

The light from the fire made it easier to spot guards on the wall, but hitting them was almost impossible. It was starting to feel hopeless and she realized she had started rationing her arrows. But there was one guard that was making a mistake. Myree could see a bit of her back just above the wall and had been watching her for the last two minutes. She would move, wait a few seconds as if gathering her courage, then pop up and fire an arrow before dropping back down. But it was too consistent. Myree was watching the pattern repeat when an arrow hit the tree trunk only ten centimeters from her left ear sending wood chips flying against her cheek.

The arrowhead disappeared into the bark and the whole tree vibrated with the impact. She dropped down and out of sight in a panic with her back against the trunk. Someone had been aiming specifically at her and almost succeeded. She thought of the guard on the wall and wondered if she had been making the same mistake herself. Was she being predictable? She didn't think so, but maybe she was. She would have to make sure not to repeat herself. Her breathing was too fast; she wouldn't be able to shoot straight. Closing her eyes, she focused on slowing down her heartbeat, breathing and racing thoughts. She imagined sitting on the ledge on the mesa with Kraster and Ena, just enjoying the sunset.

"You okay over there?" She glanced over at Bend, who looked worried, then closed her eyes again to finish.

"I'm fine. Just a close call. I need to calm down or I'll just be wasting arrows."

"Myree, you can head to the back. In fact, I wish you would."

It was such a tempting offer. She wanted to take it but she'd never forgive herself if she snuck away when everyone else stayed to fight. "No, I'll stay. This is important."

Bend nodded like he understood but didn't like it, then turned his focus back to the wall. Myree did the same but a plan began to form in her mind. She would twist to her left and peek out until she saw the predictable guard move, then she would wait a few seconds and swing out on the right side of the tree trunk to fire at the spot where she knew the guard would stand. She would finally get one of them while being unpredictable herself.

Myree readied her arrow and peered carefully around the trunk for the expected movement. There it was! Myree silently counted to five and then rolled out to her right, aimed at the spot where the larren would stand, and released the shot. As hoped, the guard stood and pulled back her own bow, but then she cried out in pain and dropped back out of sight.

She'd done it! But at almost the exact moment that she realized what she'd done, an arrow sliced past her side, piercing her shirt, cutting into her skin, and landing in the dirt behind her. Again, she was back on the ground with her back to the tree trunk. It was too dark to get a good look at her wound, but she could tell it wasn't serious. It was bleeding though and she applied pressure as she considered her situation. Someone had been waiting to take that shot at her, probably the same guard who barely missed last time. They had been watching and waiting to take their shot too. Myree felt a new fear seep through her body. She'd never felt anything like it before. It was a fear of who she could become if she just went along with what everyone else was doing. Was she a killer? Had she killed that guard? Maybe she was only injured. She tried to make herself believe that she had only injured the guard on the wall, but it was a hollow trick. She didn't know. She did know that she had tried to kill the guard whatever the outcome might be. It had all been so fun during target practice over the last week. She'd thought she was ready, but now she felt sick. She could imagine the damage her arrow must have done. She was scared to move. Two close calls; the second closer than the first.

"Bend, I hit a guard a second ago."

"What? Nice job! I keep missing."

"I feel horrible. I think I killed her."

"Just stay there. You don't have to shoot anymore."

Inside Rreker, the bell started ringing again. It sounded louder this time. Maybe it was a call for help and some of the guards on the wall would have to leave to go help. It was hard to tell and she was scared to look. Another arrow ripped a gouge in the tree she was hiding behind. It was a shot designed to hit someone peering around a tree trunk. She should make a run for it now before they could line up another shot, but she sat frozen in place. She didn't know what to do. Her side hurt and she focused on the pain to purge the other images from her mind. It didn't work. She could see herself calculating the shot; aiming to kill. She could hear the cry of pain and her imagination filled in details she hadn't seen.

CHAPTER THIRTY EIGHT

ROAR

IT WAS MIDNIGHT and Kraster stood at the edge of the Mesa staring down at the spot where he knew Rreker should be. In all his planning with Cindl, they never considered the possibility of a blanket of clouds. It was such a rare event that it simply hadn't come up. He strained his eyes looking for any hint of a fire.

"Kraster, sit down. You need to conserve your energy anyway." His dad sat near the edge beside his mom. They were surrounded by almost five hundred pairs.

'I can't. I'm too nervous. I'd just stand up again in twenty seconds."

Kraster looked along the edge on both sides. So many humans and larrens willing to take this risk with him. Were they all crazy? Were his mom and dad crazy? When he arrived at the edge an hour ago and saw the clouds he knew they were in trouble. This would be more dangerous than he had described it to everyone. It might be impossible. If the clouds went all the way to the ground, they would all crash. So far, the pairs weren't leaving as he'd expected, but everything felt thin and brittle. One loud human or larren could probably scare everyone back home.

"You see anything Dad?"

"Maybe. Over there. Are the clouds a little brighter in that spot?"

"I think you're right. It looks like they have a fire going. That means we have to go."

"We don't have to."

"They've exposed themselves and they'll probably take actions that assume we're coming. I'm going. Can you talk Mom into staying?"

"We already decided. If you go, we're going too."

"Dad, Myree and I can just climb back when this is over."

"This is a war Kraster, we don't know if any of us will come back."

Kraster felt a flush of anger. Of course he knew that, he just didn't want to talk about it. There were four hundred seventy-six pairs ready to make the jump tonight. Almost all of the humans signed up after his mom. If she hadn't stepped up, there would be a lot fewer of them ready tonight. He still didn't want her to go. Yesterday, he shared the plan for a second wave. He'd been hiding at Mennow's house all week so everyone was surprised to see him. He explained that Cindl had made the jump instead to prove adults could do it. Ena's rescue had triggered the idea, but fortunately their crash reinforced the general view that adults were too heavy. Since almost all the teenagers who wanted to go had glided down in the first wave, King Marik would never expect a second wave. But even with witnesses that Cindl had made it and lit the signal fires, getting more humans to volunteer was harder than expected. His mom was the catalyst. She announced that her daughter was down there and she was going after her. A lot of other parents were in the same situation.

Finding more larrens had been easy. There were more larren than human volunteers for the first wave and they were thrilled to have a second chance. He'd asked his old friend Mennow to be his pair and the two of them had been planning the details all week. Among larrens, light colored fur on the chest and belly was generally considered beautiful, but for a night jump it was a liability. The plan was to organized the line up so the darkest colored larrens would jump first and the lighter colored larrens would jump last. If it worked, most of them would be on the ground by the time a light-colored larren was noticed.

The spot his dad pointed out was more obvious now. It glowed like globelight under a thin blanket. He couldn't imagine Cindl lighting the fire if the clouds reached the ground. She would know that was hopeless. Unless she'd been captured and their plan discovered. For all he knew, it might be a random house fire. He longed for certainty, or even well-defined probability.

"Listen up everyone. We have our signal fire so I'm going down. Obviously this isn't what any of you signed up for. No one in their right mind would expect you to follow me without being able to see the ground." Kraster could feel the cracks spreading through his own confidence. He'd given everyone an honorable exit. He shouldn't have done that, but he couldn't help it. "If you decide to follow me, make sure the globelights on your backs are shaken. They won't do us any good in the clouds, but we'll still need them to follow each other for most of the way down. I forgot to ask, are you still willing to go Mennow?"

"Yeah, I'm going."

"Okay, there's no shame in backing out, but if you still want to go, form up into three lines; one behind Mennow and I and then one on either side of us. We'll jump first, then the first pairs in each of the lines should jump five seconds later. Then after that, just keep the five second pace going until everyone who wants to is on their way down. Light colored larrens in the back like we talked about earlier. Hopefully it won't matter, but we only get one chance at this. Okay, line up."

Kraster watched almost everyone line up with a sense of dread. They weren't using their heads; they were just following his lead; assuming he knew what he was doing. He couldn't force his parents to stay behind, but he'd deliberately paired them with light colored larrens to make sure they were near the back of the line. It was a small hope, but maybe the larren his mom was paired with would change his mind.

They'd seen the fire fifteen minutes ago. The plan was to wait fifteen minutes before they jumped so it was time to go. He wished for something more substantial than his small knife, but they couldn't risk the extra weight. If Cindl did her job, the resistance would have weapons waiting for them when they landed.

Mennow stepped closer the edge. Kraster could tell he was terrified, and for the first time that night Kraster was scared for himself. He'd been so focused on everyone else, especially his mom. Now he was physically at the edge. He was excited for the initial jump; he remembered how exciting it had been the first time. But those clouds. The thought of gliding blind made his stomach turn.

Kraster put his hand on Mennow's shoulder. "We better go before I back out."

"You're scared too? That makes me feel a little better. I was feeling like a coward."

"A coward? I don't think anyone will ever call you a coward for the rest of your life, Mennow. You ready?"

"I think so."

Mennow shuffled forward and crouched down for his jump while Kraster stretched out his hands. In the next moment they were falling into the darkness with Kraster yelling into the wind. It was hard to describe how frightening and incredible it felt and he considered climbing back up in the future just to do it again. They leveled out and glided down toward the cloud cover. He couldn't see the flames, but the rising smoke was breaking through the glowing clouds. He stole a glance back but couldn't see anyone. That was silly; the whole point of doing this at night was so that they couldn't be seen, but not being able to see anyone behind him was unnerving. Maybe no one had followed him. There was no point considering it. The rope was snug and Mennow was wearing the glass mask they'd built during the week. Glass was a rare commodity on the mesa so they only made one, but at least Mennow should be able to see and everyone else was following him. The other pairs would have to take turns keeping their eyes open, but at least they knew what to expect.

They dropped into the clouds and he could feel the moisture build on his skin and seep into his clothes. They dropped steadily trying not to alter their course and hoping they weren't drifting one direction or the other. And then the clouds broke and they could see Rreker below them. If his heart had been beating fast, it started beating faster. The fire shot into the sky like the perfect beacon and illuminated the whole center circle that stretched out in front of it. Perfect. The center circle was almost empty which made sense as the sound of battle drifted up to him. He'd never seen Rreker from the air, but it was magnificent. The center circle looked smaller than he remembered, but that was probably just because he was looking at it surrounded by the larger city. The main radial streets each shot off from the center toward the eight gates. The buildings were larger and taller near the center and occasionally along the main radials, but most of the city was full of smaller homes and was dotted with darker colored patches that he guessed must be parks. He'd never seen one of the parks on his trip through the city. They'd drifted a little to their left but nothing serious and Mennow instantly corrected course.

Kraster glanced back one last time, but this time he could see three pairs close behind him silhouetted against the clouds and one more dropped through as he watched. Mennow steered toward the middle of the circle with all of Myree's landing instructions racing through his head.

The resistance fighters on the edge of the circle saw them drop out of the cloud cover and ran out into the circle. The original plan was to wait until the pairs started landing but that was based on the assumption that they wouldn't be able to see them coming. The illuminated cloud cover served as a reddish-white background that made the gliding pairs obvious to anyone paying attention. They had to adapt. Kraster hoped most of them could land before King Marik's guards saw them coming, but even before Mennow touched the ground, a bell in the palace started ringing and palace guards started running into the circle. So much for landing in secret; they would be landing in the middle of a battle. The resistance advanced on the palace guard trying to keep the circle open for landings.

Mennow landed hard almost exactly in the center of the circle, but didn't fall and roll.

"Great landing!" There wasn't a hint of sarcasm in Kraster's voice. He pulled out his small knife and cut the rope that was holding him against Mennow's back. "You okay?"

"I'm good."

"Okay. I'll help the first wave get clear then I'll join you at the north end."

Mennow limped as quickly as he could toward the north end of the circle. Kraster scanned the landing zone. He should have spaced them out more, but the circle was big enough that everyone was instinctively spreading out on the final approach looking for open ground. Fifty meters toward the palace he spotted a crashed pair and ran to help. The larren was in pain but the rider was dead. Even knowing this could happen, Kraster struggled to accept it. He cut the rope and pulled the body to the side. What could he do for the man? There was nothing he could do, but just leaving him there felt wrong. The larren's cries focused his attention, but he didn't know what to do for him.

'Kraster! Are you hurt?" Cindl was running toward him.

"Cindl! I'm so glad you're here." She gave him a quick hug and looked him over. "Yeah, I'm fine. That man's dead and this larren's hurt."

"I'll take care of the larren. I need you to keep the plan on track." The bell continued to ring in the background and Kraster noticed it again wondering why more guards weren't pouring into the circle.

"We rang the bell earlier. False alarm of course, so we're hoping most of the guards at the walls will ignore it this time."

"Brilliant. Was that your idea?"

"No, it was Ena's idea."

"Is she here?"

"Somewhere, yeah. Not sure where though. Okay, go. We'll talk later."

Kraster watched the battle for a moment between the resistance and palace guard. There were more guards than he'd guessed and a small but steady stream of reinforcements was trickling in from all sides. It was one more decision he didn't want to make. They had to get a gate open so he knew what they should do, but it would mean more good larrens and humans would die in the circle. The stream of pairs was still gliding in and he guessed his parents hadn't landed yet but he didn't know. He started running toward the north end of the circle.

"This way! Come on. We'll come back and help here, but we have to get the north gate open."

There was already a group gathered at the north end of the circle and the group following Kraster doubled the size. One of the largest larrens Kraster had ever seen was waiting for him. Kraster nodded at him, giving him permission to take over.

"Everyone follow me." The larren's voice easily carried over the sounds of war, then he ran out of the circle toward the north gate.

The resistance had a pile of swords and bows off to the side and Kraster quickly picked out a sword that wasn't too heavy for him. Just ahead, Mennow was trying to run but his leg couldn't handle it.

"Mennow, stay here and keep directing anyone you can to follow us to the north gate. I think it's just straight up this street. We might need help so try to keep them coming."

"Okay, I'll do that." Mennow looked relieved to have a job he could perform well.

Kraster sprinted to catch up with the group but he was still at the back when they reached the gate. The larren in front didn't stop to scout or plan, he just charged at the closest guard and without a chance to prepare, the war started in earnest for Kraster. A woman fell beside him with only seconds left to live but he felt an armor wrapping around his mind. If he reacted to the horror, let it distract him, he'd be dead too. So he fought - hard. He fell into the mindset with surprising ease. When a guard was trying to kill him, he tried to kill them first. Then it didn't matter if they attacked him first. He knew they would if they could so he attacked first. Five minutes later they were opening the north gate. Every one of King Marik's guards was dead and about half of Kraster's group was dead too.

As soon as the gate opened, humans and larrens surged in. The resistance had quietly made sure that the biggest and fastest among them were at the north gate. Kraster recognized most of the Wall and Hammer players mixed in with the resistance larrens. Everyone was yelling and cheering and slapping Kraster's back.

"Let's split in half. I'll lead a group back to the circle to go after King Marik. The rest of you hit the next gate. Sound good? If you're coming with me, this way." Kraster shouted the instructions and started moving. The half closest to him split off and followed. He was tired but he wanted to run. Mennow had been sending pairs toward them and they were absorbed into the growing crowd. The army he was leading was powerful; he could hear its size and bulk as they ran down the street and broke into the circle. That feeling of power flooded his own mind and he sped up from a jog to an easy run. They were like a water drop sliding down a roof getting bigger and faster as it absorbs smaller drops. The resistance fighters were just ahead and clearly being beaten. Kraster couldn't help sprinting now. His sword was pointed at the sky and his army roared as it smashed into the palace guards.

CHAPTER THIRTY NINE

POISON AND POWER

THE BELL WAS still ringing inside Rreker but now they could also hear the sound of fighting on the other side of the wall. Myree risked a quick glance around the tree but couldn't see anyone on the wall. Off to her right, the core of their little army broke out of the trees for another attempt on the gate. They must have noticed the same thing.

"Myree, they need cover." Bend was firing arrows as fast as he could at the wall trying to make anyone up there think twice about standing up.

She made herself stand but her legs felt stiff. Was this different? She was trying to protect the lives of her friends. It was motivated by her best impulses. She readied an arrow and moved to aim at the wall. It felt like she was moving in thick syrup as her mind wrestled with her muscle memory. She pulled back the string, hearing the bow creak with horrible power. She released and the arrow flew at the wall. She hadn't aimed at anyone. She repeated the motions, a little easier this time. She aimed at random spots along the wall hoping no one accidentally stood.

She could hear cheering inside the gate and then it opened outward. The resistance and diggers outside crouched in anticipation, then stood and start cheering too.

"Come on!" Bend's face was jubilant. "I know those guys. They must have broken through the North Gate."

Bend started running toward the crowd glancing over his shoulder to make sure Myree was following. There was more war inside the gate; she knew that. The thought of it coursed through her like a poison and her jaw was clenched so tight that her teeth hurt when she finally opened her mouth. She tried to relax as she jogged toward the crowd. If she walked Bend would come back and she couldn't talk right now. She didn't know what to do or think, so she followed, hoping it would give her time to decide.

By the time she made it to the gate, the combined army was already moving toward the next one. The bodies of lifeless humans and larrens were spread out across the wide courtyard just inside the gate. It was the most horrible thing she'd ever seen, worse than anything her imagination had ever supplied. She stopped involuntarily, shocked by the loss; the evil of so much inflicted suffering and death. Then her mind drifted up to the wall behind her now. The guard she shot was up there. She would be dead now, even if someone else delivered the final stroke. If she could see the body; see that someone else was the killer, maybe she'd feel better. As soon as the thought entered her mind she knew it wouldn't work. There was no way to shift her guilt onto someone else.

Something held her in that place. This was important. It was changing her as she stood there. Myree swallowed, wiped tears out of her eyes and turned slowly in a circle, absorbing the brutality of it. She stopped turning when she recognized a larren resistance fighter from the march to Rreker. Three nights ago, he sang a beautiful old love song. She'd heard it before, but you could tell the words meant something to him. The next day in the supper line, he'd known her name. "Careful Myree, the soup's still really hot." It surprised her at the time but then she dismissed it; almost everyone knew her name. Now it mattered again. His eyes stared stupidly into space. In addition to the fear and shock, she felt anger. No one would ever hear his rich calming voice again. Someone had swung a sword and killed him. Someone like herself. She wanted to turn and run away, and she wanted to stay and close his eyes; to squeeze a drop of dignity from this terrible place. Her mind was torn in two, so her feet decided for her, carrying her quietly toward her fallen comrade. She knelt beside him and closed his eyes with her fingers.

She stood to leave but there were so many more. Moving from one to the next, she closed their eyes and covered them as best she could. It was only after she was halfway through that she realized the commitment she'd made. She would have to face her guard. A few minutes later, she was at the stairs leading up to the top of the wall. She climbed as if condemned. Each step was heavy and her chest was tight. Then she moved along the wall, taking care of each larren until she came to the one she feared the most. She was lying on her side, Myree's arrow buried deep and her eyes half open. She didn't bother wiping her eyes now, it was pointless. There was no other sign of injury she could see. No chance to even share this guilt. She gently closed the guard's eyes, more carefully than all the others.

Myree made her way back down to the courtyard and followed a street into the city. All the fighting seemed to be along the wall and she wanted to be alone. Everyone loved to talk about how fearless she was; how she would attack a full grown larren. But they were completely missing who she was. That attack didn't happen because she was fearless. She'd done it to survive and out of desperation. To be fearless seemed vicious, and she wasn't vicious. Or maybe to be more honest, she didn't want to be vicious. Would her brother be okay with all this? Was Bend swinging a sword right now? Would her mom tell her it was okay? But it didn't matter what they thought - she wasn't okay with this. No one forced her to shoot her arrow at that guard. It had been her decision. Everyone would say this was for a noble cause; to overthrow a cruel king and free thousands of human slaves. She would have said it herself an hour ago. Could there have been another way? She didn't know, but she wished she'd looked harder before this all started.

The night still flickered as the building continued to burn in the middle of Rreker. It was quieter though. The next gate must have fallen and the surge moved on to the next one further around. A breeze carried in the scent of the forest. It smelled so good, so peaceful, so out of place. The sounds from far away suggested chaos and loudness, but the street was still and quiet. It felt wrong, like this isolated place was naively at peace when no one should feel peaceful. After several minutes she found a small park with trees around the edges and gardens in the middle. It would be beautiful in sunlight and it was like an embrace in the darkness. She found a bench and sat down. With her eyes closed, she could hear the sound of moving branches, rustling leaves and the impact of distant swords.

Myree heard footsteps and then a quiet voice. "You can make it. We're almost there."

Two larrens stumbled into the park and Myree was on her

feet with an arrow to her cheek faster than she'd thought possible. The larrens froze and stared at her in the weak firelight, unsure what to do. The string slipped a little in her tired fingers and she lowered her aim to be safe.

"I'm not going to shoot you. You'd better hide until this is over." The larrens hesitated, unsure if this was a trick; if she was toying with them. "I'm serious. They'll kill you if they find you right now."

"I can't run anymore." The second larren stood for a few more seconds, then awkwardly sank into the grass and Myree noticed the wet glistening of blood on his face and back.

If there had been poison flowing through Myree before, it was flushed away by something new. Something powerful that stirred up from the deepest parts of her. She didn't know what to call it, but she knew what she would do. Everyone else in the whole world could say this slaughter was right, but she knew it was wrong. At the core of her being, she knew it.

"Don't worry. Lie still. I'm going to protect you."

CHAPTER FORTY
WOUNDED

Kraster sat on the ground with his back against the outside wall of an old house. The group of humans and larrens he'd been fighting beside for the last two hours was spread out around him. The first hour had been exhausting but then the pace slowed down. The wall was breached, King Marik captured, and Kraster's army surged through the city hunting down the remaining pockets of Marik's guards.

A young human boy ran around the corner and pulled up short when he saw them. "Is Kraster here?" From the way he was dressed Kraster guessed he was a recently freed slave.

"Yeah, I'm Kraster."

"I'm supposed to find you, Sir. Your Mom's hurt."

"Where is she?" Kraster stood as did everyone else in the group.

"Follow me, I'll take you."

Kraster could feel his breath catch in his throat; like something in his chest shrank and all the muscles around it tightened up in response.

"Hold on Kraster, this could be a trap." It was Jenik from the tunnel camp and he was right.

"Well if it is, it's a great one. I have to check it out."

"We'll come with you until we're sure."

Kraster forced himself to breathe and run, following the nameless boy down the unfamiliar streets. He was leading a small portion of his army, but there was no sense of power this time. Everything was a blur as he cycled through the list of possible injuries. He tried to focus his energy on running faster. They crossed the center circle, headed down a main radial, turned onto a smaller side street, finally stopping at a long single story building. It had been converted into a field hospital and there was a steady trickle of humans and larren coming in and out - some needing help and some having received it.

"She's in there, sir."

"Thank you." Kraster turned back to his friends, "Thanks for coming. I don't think this is a trap." Several nodded their agreement. He nodded back his appreciation and walked into the hospital.

The whole place was in chaos. He could tell from the way some of the beds were lined up that there had originally been some order and structure, but two hours of war had killed it. The neat matrix of beds had collapsed with so many humans and larrens filling in every available space. He saw Cindl before he saw his mother.

"Is she okay?"

"I think she'll be okay, Kraster, but she lost consciousness a few minutes ago."

"What happened?" Kraster dropped to his knees beside

her bed, instinctively holding her hand and lightly touching her hair.

"I wasn't with her, but I recognized her when they carried her past me. I heard they were surprised from behind." Cindl pointed at a larren lying on a mat only four patients over from his Mom. "She hit your Mom with a club and then fell on her after being injured herself."

"Which one? Over there?"

"Kraster, calm down. She was injured much worse than your Mom; I doubt she'll make it until daylight."

"I'm going to kill her."

"Kraster! Stop. Listen to me. We started a war. A WAR!" Cindl's voice faltered with suppressed tension and she paused to recover. "For the last few hours we've been trying to kill or injure them and they've been trying to do the same to us. It's still happening out there right now. Your Mom was trying to kill that larren and the soldiers with her probably succeeded. We'll know soon. This whole thing is so much worse than I imagined."

"Cindl, if someone tried to kill you, I'd try to kill them, and I'll bet you'd do the same for me."

"It's not that simple. When this is over, we all have to live together. If we were fighting beside each other and someone tried to kill you, then yes, of course I'd try to kill them first. But once they're injured and not a threat, it changes. It has to change. Otherwise this can never end until everyone on one side or the other is dead."

Kraster grunted a grudging acknowledgment.

"Kraster. Hey, look at me. I have to go. I stayed with your Mom until you, Myree or your Dad could get here, but I have to go try to stop the fighting."

"Where's my dad? He wouldn't have left her."

"I don't know. They must have been separated. Kraster, it's obvious we won. There's no point in any more death. Stay with your Mom. I'll come back as soon as I can. And don't touch that larren. She deserves as much respect and care as your Mom does. Kraster, I'm serious. Don't touch that larren."

"I won't."

Cindl gripped his arm, gave him a look something between a reassuring smile and a warning, then moved off through the crowded noisy room. The weight of the war, his war, seemed to drift down from the ceiling and drape itself over his head and shoulders. He sat down on the floor and looked at his mom's dirty face. He could see the streaks where her tears had run out of the corners of her eyes. This was not supposed to happen. Others could get hurt or die; he even knew it could happen to him. But not his Mom. Not his Dad or Myree. Not Cindl or Bend or Ena. After a short search he found some supplies and gently cleaned her face and neck. A doctor had given her something for the pain but they hadn't been able to spend any time on her yet. Evidently there were others who needed attention more urgently.

He stood and walked to where the injured larren lay on the ground. She had been hastily bandaged but no one was helping her now. She groaned and tried to move but the only result was that one of the bandages on her back came loose and a deep cut started bleeding again. He looked around but there was no one else to help her. His Mom had tried to kill this larren and this larren had tried to kill his Mom. Now they both lay helpless in a horrible hospital that was still surrounded by war. He knelt beside her and tried to stick the bandage back in place without touching her. He didn't want to touch her.

But it wouldn't work. The bandage was soaked and needed to be replaced. There was a stack of bandages next to her and he started cutting one to size. His body shook, overcome with emotion, as he removed the old bandage, cleaned the wound and covered it with a fresh bandage.

"Thank you." Her voice was so quiet he almost missed it. She couldn't see him; she was facing the other direction. He wondered if she would have said that if she knew who he was.

"Forgive me."

CHAPTER FORTY ONE

UNOPPOSED

Myree was lying on her back on the roof of their new barn. The sun was bright overhead and she was squinting her eyes to get just the right shade of red glowing through her eyelids. Cindl was sitting beside her enjoying the long break and finishing a bread roll from earlier. They'd been working all morning and would probably be working most of the afternoon, but the roof was half finished and it looked great. Kraster and her dad built the frame earlier in the week, but Cindl had volunteered to put on the roof and Myree jumped to help. It was built back against the wall of the canyon so that it would be in the cool shade during the afternoons. For now, the sun was pleasantly warm with the steady breeze blowing in from the desert.

There had been a big rain up on the mesa overnight which meant the riverbed was full of water for the first time since she'd moved out to the canyon with her family. It sounded smooth as it glided over the sand and stone. Myree listened to the river of air flowing up the canyon and the river of water flowing down the canyon. The observation made her happy and she allowed her lips to tilt into a smile.

It was the second time Cindl had come out to visit in the three months since the war ended and Myree loved her visits. Cindl didn't seem as damaged by the war as the rest of her family. At least she didn't seem scared that it would come up in a conversation. Even without all that, she just liked her.

"I forgot how much I love it out here." Cindl's voice made Myree jump, which made them both laugh, but Myree kept her eyes closed.

"I love it too. Are you going to move out here with us? It's your house after all."

"No. Your family needs to be a family again for a while. I'm a bit of a complication. Besides, I feel needed in Rreker for now."

"I think my Mom would be happy to have you join us. Ena already lives with us obviously, and Bend's only twenty minutes up the canyon."

Cindl seemed pleased. "Your Mom invited me last time I was here, and again this morning. Maybe I will someday. You're the closest thing I have to a family."

"I almost forgot. You could climb back up to your family couldn't you?"

"I could. Let's just say my reunion wasn't as great as yours was. In theory I could visit, but I'm terrified to glide back down again. Twice is enough for me and I like it down here so much better."

"I didn't know things were bad with your family."

"It wasn't horrible, but it didn't even come close to what I imagined. I think we were just apart for too long. We didn't know each other and we didn't need each other anymore."

Cindl ended with a tone that suggested that was all she'd like to say.

"Is the rebuilding still going well in Rreker?"

"Yeah, it is. I know I've said this before, but having something we can all work on together is probably the best cure I can think of. I suppose it isn't a cure, but it's helping."

"And King Marik? Is he still causing problems?"

Cindl laughed. "He was! We've basically had to end all visitations. Even with guards monitoring the visits he would still manage to get messages out to his followers. Fortunately, he doesn't have many left, but there's enough that they can be disruptive. I can't tell you how many times I've wished he died in the war."

"He doesn't get to see anyone anymore?"

"No. Well, he shares a cell with his two generals. They're going to get really tired of each other."

Several minutes of comfortable silence passed between them. Neither of them was ready to get back to work and the weather was almost perfect for September. "Did you plant all these fruit trees?"

"Most of them, yes. There were a few nearby when I got here. I didn't plant them all at once, but I planted a handful every year and the next thing I knew I had an orchard!" She paused, but it was obvious she was getting ready to say something else. "Alright Myree, I've got a question for you that I'm worried might be a sore subject. I can't come up with a graceful way to bring it up, so I'd like to just dive in with your permission."

"You have my permission to potentially offend me."

That elicited a chuckle. "I'd rather not. But since you offered... You decided pretty quick that you weren't going to have any more to do with the war, but everyone else you care about kept fighting. I haven't heard you say anything about it, but when I try to put myself in your place, I think it would really bother me. Are you doing okay?"

Myree squinted her eyes open to peer over at Cindl, then propped herself up on her elbows. "No one else has asked me about that. It has been bothering me. It helps that no one close to me is bragging about what they did. Before we left Rreker it was harder; with everyone talking about their portion of the heroics. Everyone in my family seems pretty miserable. Well, not Mom. She came out of it all in the worst shape but she's the happiest in our family."

"She got something back that she thought she'd lost forever. She deserves to be happy."

"I think so too."

"We got a little off topic."

"Yeah we did." Myree sat up all the way and folded her hands in her lap. "If I hadn't killed a guard myself, I think it'd be harder, but I did the same thing."

"No, it was different. All of us started fighting, but you reacted differently than the rest of us. We kept going. You stopped."

"I took a few more shots at the wall. I don't think I hit anyone, but what if I had?" She looked at Cindl who didn't look convinced. "You're right. I don't know why I reacted so differently. I wish someone else had too. You tried to stop the war…"

"Only after it was obvious we won. Completely different."

Myree's voice was softer when the spoke again. "I hate that everyone I love killed so many larrens. I know they were trying to do something good, but it still makes me feel alone; like we picked different sides. I don't know if that will go away or if I'm stuck with it."

"You make us uncomfortable, Myree. The rest of us think back on what we did and we wonder if we were wrong. Our intentions were good as you said, but once the war started there was so much momentum to fight. I've used that as an excuse, but that's hard when I know you were in the same current, but you planted your feet and stood against it. I wish I'd reacted the way you did."

"You do?"

"I do. And I'm not the only one. People talk about you a lot back in Rreker."

"Yeah, the traitor Myree. I remember."

"There's still a lot of that too, but you'd be amazed. You're a traitor to some and a hero to others."

Myree started to say something but stopped. She suddenly didn't feel as alone. "Thanks for telling me."

"You're welcome."

"Is everyone still calling it Kraster's War? He hates that."

"I'm afraid so. You're a hero to one group and Kraster's a hero to the rest. It's kind of funny. It does seem like you two should be at each other's throats, but I've been out here enough to see that's not true."

"No. I wish so badly that he'd done things differently, but in a strange way, I feel closer to him than before the war. Ena has this great expression: we can't get rid of evil in the world, but we can make sure it isn't unopposed. I love that. It describes Kraster perfectly, and that's who I want to be too."

"That sounds like both of you to me."

CHAPTER FORTY TWO

FORGIVENESS

THE MORNING WAS still cold but at least it was calm. The rising sun hadn't had enough time to build up a noticeable breeze. Kraster and his mom walked slowly along the riverbed. As usual, they walked in silence away from the house; conversation would come later. She was doing much better, but still held his arm for support. "In case I trip", she would say. Her limp was less pronounced than it was even a month ago, but she still had to move slowly to minimize the pain. Kraster was always tired when they started, but everything about the early morning walks stirred the senses. This morning the cold air pinched their faces and the Three Sisters shone brighter than normal in the morning sky just above the canyon rim.

Kraster loved and hated these walks. He loved his mom and would do anything for her, but this little tradition forced her injury and his guilt to the surface over and over. In the six months since the war, she'd never brought it up. She seemed sincerely happy just to be with him. Kraster never brought it up either, but every morning the tension ticked higher; his mom's contentment and his anguish.

"Do you think we could try to get up to the rim this morning? I've been eyeing that path by the bend for a couple weeks. I think I can make it. It's not very steep."

"Sure Mom. If you want to try it, I'll help you."

"I really do. I love the canyon, but sometimes it feels like I'm looking at the world through a window. I want to see the whole mesa and the whole desert."

A few minutes later they were moving slowly up the trail. It was the easiest way to the rim, but it was still much steeper than their normal walks. Although she worked to hide it, Kraster could tell from her face that these vertical steps hurt. And now that they'd started, Kraster remembered the one steep section further up. This was foolish. Although most of the trail was easy, he knew she wouldn't be able to scramble up that section and he would have to watch her try and fail. As they moved closer, Kraster's nervousness built in his chest. Finally, the obstacle came into clear view and they stopped to look at it.

"Oh my. It looked easier from the bottom. I think I'll sit and rest for a minute."

They sat on a large rock beside each other facing back down into the canyon. The sound of moving leaves rose and fell as the first gusts of the morning breeze rolled past them up the canyon.

"Kraster, I'm embarrassed to ask, but would you carry me up past this section. I think I can make it the rest of the way myself."

"Mom…" His voice cracked under the strain. "You shouldn't have to ask for help! How can you not hate me?"

Kraster turned away and tried to breathe slowly and deeply. His throat was tight and his muscles tensed.

The suddenness of his emotion surprised her, but they had been circling this conversation for months and there was that heightened sense of awareness that comes when something long-feared finally begins. "You didn't do this to me."

"I did! If you hadn't followed me down, you'd be fine right now."

"If I hadn't chosen to follow you. You forgot that I chose to follow you. You were against it as I recall."

"But I put you in a position where you had to make that choice, and if I was you, I would have felt forced to do the same thing."

"Life is full of choices that we wish we didn't have to make, but we still make them. I don't regret it, Kraster. You do; we can all see that, but I made a decision I'm proud of. I don't know how to say this without bragging, but that was the bravest things I've ever done. I was so scared. It was honorable and selfless in so many ways. Don't take that away from me by claiming you forced me to follow."

"I don't want to… But Mom, look how much it's cost you. If I could…", Kraster paused one last time to consider the weight of the words, "if I could make a trade somehow - my life in that war to keep you from getting hurt - I'd do it. I hate myself for coming up with that stupid plan. If I…" But he couldn't finish. He was like a man sliding down a steep embankment. Initially he'd fought to regain control, but now he knew he couldn't arrest the slide and he allowed it to happen. He felt his mom take his hand in both of hers as he trembled and ached. She kissed it and moved closer to him on the rock.

Her voice was strained too, but she spoke with a firmness that cut through his storm and made itself heard.

"But I would never accept the trade. Never." She waited for her words to settle then continued. "I had a hard time hearing your speech on the mesa. It forced me to confront the fact that I was wallowing in hatred too. I probably would've denied it, but I was. It was different for me than it was for you. You had so many larrens to hate, but all my hatred centered on Wilton. Someday, I hope you start your own family, and when you do, you'll understand how deeply he hurt me. I just wanted to be your mother. To help you with your school work, or take care of you when you were sick. Tell you stories, or even better, hear the stories you would have come up with. He ripped that all away from me and I hated him. I've never hated anyone more. I would give almost anything to have those years back. But I can't have them. There's no deal I can make."

Kraster remained bent over with his head bowed. She stroked his hair, her voice calmer now. "It was eating me up inside, even after I knew he was dead. But the only way I could move on was to forgive him. He couldn't apologize and I don't know if he deserves forgiveness, but I needed to forgive him. I was stuck until I did. I see you trying to move on but you're stuck. I think you might be able to forgive everyone else, but you can't forgive yourself."

"So you admit I need to be forgiven. I'm guilty."

"No, that's not what I meant! You were trying to do something good. I'm proud of you."

"But the result was death and suffering. You almost died Mom!"

"Kraster, no. You're trying to carry all of this, but you're not to blame. You're my son. Nine thousand human slaves were freed because of that war."

"And another three thousand were killed before we could free them. They would still be alive."

They sat silently considering each other's words. The Three Sisters had all but disappeared in the brightening sky and the beginnings of a steady wind stirred in the canyon. The sun finally broke above the mesa and flooded the canyon with light and clarity.

"I guess we all carry some guilt for this war. I helped kill five larrens before almost being killed myself. After it was over I asked around. I only found out who one of them was, but she was a teacher. She loved cooking."

"You never would have done it if I hadn't… Don't you see? It all comes back to me in the end."

"Those deaths, including the human and larren fighters on both sides - those deaths are on all of us. You proposed a plan that we could have rejected, but we didn't. We embraced it. We cheered when you spoke."

"You're trying to convince me that I'm not responsible for this - for you - but I know I am. Because of what I did, what I decided to do, I hurt you."

All her emotions screamed to say no; to shift the blame away from her son. She wanted to argue and clarify his words, but she understood now what they both needed. She allowed herself to see his guilt and her heart broke. She didn't want to forgive him because she wanted him to be innocent.

"Kraster, you're not responsible for everything that happened, but you're right, some portion of the guilt is yours." She choked back the urge to elaborate and soften the blow, but she knew she had to let the words stand. "And Kraster, I forgive you for your part in hurting me."

Kraster leaned against her now crying harder but different tears. They rested for a long time in this new peace between them. Finally, she shifted beside him.

"I want you to know, I would give up my ability to walk in a heartbeat for this second chance to be your mom. I'm happy! I want you to be happy too."

"I'll try."

"Now, are you going to help me get to the rim or not?"

Kraster laughed and finally looked at his mom, then knelt down in front of her. "Climb on and hold on tight."

He climbed past the steep section and kept going, against her protests, until they reached the top. Then he knelt again to let her down.

"Thank you."

Kraster just smiled as she slowly turned, enjoying the wide horizon of desert; the massive bulk of the base and mesa. "It's beautiful. Would you bring me back up here to watch the sunset?"

"I'd love to."

CHAPTER FORTY THREE
JADIN MOUNTAINS

"MYREE, CHECK THIS out!"

"Where are you?"

"Over here. If you reach around the rock to your right, you should be able to find the handhold. I see your arm. A little higher. There you go. You got it."

"Wow! What is that?"

"No idea. It's too round to be a cave. Too perfectly round."

"At least, not like any cave we've ever seen before. Have you gone inside yet?"

"Nope. I was waiting for you. But check this out, you wouldn't be able to see this from below. The ledge would block it. And there's no way to get to it at all from the other side. I just happened to reach around that rock on a whim and found the handhold, but with such an obvious route continuing up, there's no reason to even look over here."

"What are you getting at, Kraster?"

"I don't know. That's just what popped into my head. I suppose, I'm saying that if I hadn't reached around that rock, this would probably be hidden here for hundreds of years."

"Thousands."

"Why would someone who could make this put it in a spot that probably wouldn't be found? It doesn't make sense."

"Good question. Maybe it used to be easier to get over here. You know, maybe some of the cliff broke away a long time ago."

"Yeah, I suppose. You want to go in first?" Kraster bowed his head reverently and motioned into the cave with his free hand.

"Sure. Thanks."

Myree stepped into the opening of the tunnel, or cave - whatever it was. The ceiling was about three heads taller than her and she could stand up easily, although the round ceiling coming down on either side still made her want to duck her head. She took two more steps in then stopped to let her eyes adjust after being in the bright afternoon sun only moments before.

"How deep is it?"

"I can't tell yet; my eyes are still adjusting. You coming?"

"Right behind you. Feel the sides. They're so smooth! Like someone used sandpaper to polish them."

"The ceiling too. Amazing. How would someone make this?"

"I don't know, it seems impossible. I don't think anyone could carry heavy tools up here."

"Hey, feel this part! It's an arrow. I can just make it out."

"My eyes haven't adjusted yet."

"It's an arrow carved into the ceiling pointing straight out of the tunnel. Oh wow! There's an arrow on both side walls too. They're both pointing out of the tunnel just like the one on the ceiling. Can you feel this?"

"Yeah."

Myree's pulse started racing. "Kraster! Someone carved the word 'Jadin' above the arrows. Wait, it says it next to the arrow on the ceiling too." Myree moved Kraster's hand to the right spot so he could feel the letters cut into the smooth stone. "Can you see it yet?"

"Just barely." Neither of them was ready to say what they were thinking quite yet. "I'll bet there would be another arrow on the floor if we pushed all the sand out."

"Let's try it."

Myree and Kraster started at the entrance pushing the accumulated sand out where it fell like a sand waterfall and then disappeared into the wind. It took about twenty minutes but they finally cleared the floor and as predicted there was a fourth arrow and 'Jadin' carved into the otherwise smooth floor.

They stared out across the desert in the direction indicated by the arrows, and really by the whole tunnel itself. There were no mountains to be seen on the horizon, but there was a small outcropping of rocks, barely visible, far out in the desert. The desert was littered with rock outcroppings and many were much larger and closer. But this particular one lined up perfectly with the tunnel.

"I don't know Myree, I thought they'd be bigger."

"That would be hilarious! The fabled Jadin rock pile. Well, I'm going to check it out. If you go with me that is. I don't want to go alone."

"I'm in. I'll bet Ena and Bend will join us. Mom and Dad might want to come too."

"You think Mom's up to it?"

"Probably. She's walking so much better. As long as we

don't have to do a lot of climbing. We'll go slow if we have to. I'm not sneaking off on her again."

"Me neither."

They combed the tunnel one last time before climbing back down. It was Myree that finally said something.

"The Jadin Mountains are real; not just part of our stories. Whoever lives there can carve a perfectly round tunnel high up on the cliffs."

"Let's go find them."

APPENDIX:

Cindl,

You said to let you know if I found anything really interesting in the old larren archives. This certainly qualifies. I haven't shown it to anyone else yet - I can see why it was restricted. I know you're busy, but stop by when you have a moment. We need to decide whether to release this or not.

Title
Treatise on Human Origins
Author
Unknown
Date
Estimated between 20 and 60 years after Council.

Section 13
Restricted Access
Council College Library

[Librarian's note: This is the oldest surviving work on human origin and almost none of the referenced events or documents can be separately verified. The conclusions have been deemed inflammatory.]

We have no written history prior to Mullna's account of the 2nd Water War. However, as Jelek's excellent paper last year demonstrated, there are many reasons to believe that the oral histories collected by Rinr during Queen Andl's rule are generally reliable. This allows us to look much farther back in time, albeit with less certainty. This paper will attempt to answer the question - Where did the humans come from? I have studied this topic in detail for the last twenty years and offer what I believe are the most convincing and reliable arguments. Finally, I will offer my conclusions on perhaps the most troubling question about humans - Are they smarter than us?

Starting with origins, as controversial as this view has been historically, there is almost no ambiguity in the records that the humans claimed to have come from another star system, and specifically from a planet they called Earth. Ultimately it is impossible to tell from the evidence we have whether this story is true or an elaborate story. I can only say that after two decades of study, I believe this story to be true. All the theories proposing a ruse become less likely the more they are considered, and I have not been able to conceive of a theory of my own that would explain why they would make it up.

The strongest arguments in favor of the story's veracity are as follows: 1) Both their and our stories of a grand meeting seem unlikely if we had been living together on this planet for eons. 2) Their descriptions of earth had a great deal of divergence, or variety. This would probably be the case if a large group were sharing their stories about a large planet, but is unlikely if it was all a prearranged story. 3) While it sounds like Earth was very similar to our planet in many ways, some of the descriptions are so crazy to our imagination that it is hard to imagine an indigenous species making them up, much less trying to pass them off as truth. 4) Their early behavior suggests a focus on avoiding extinction, despite their technological superiority over larrens.

Taking these in order, both larren and human stories record a grand meeting between our species, which by all accounts was orchestrated by the humans. Is it possible that humans lived and prospered on this planet for ages and we never even suspected their existence? It is true that we live on a relatively small corner of this planet and even now we don't know what lies beyond the desert. This would suggest that indeed it could be possible for our two species to have lived in ignorance of each other. However, after the Water Wars, humans occasionally wandered across the desert to us. In fact, every human living here now is descended from humans that came across the desert after the Water Wars, mostly from the large group that came 262 years after the last Water War. If they occasionally wandered across the desert after the Water War, why wouldn't they have wandered across the desert before the Grand Meeting? While I think this point is strong enough to merit mention, it is clearly the weakest argument.

Much more compelling, the divergent accounts of Earth in the oral traditions suggest a lack of premeditated collusion. In my youth I thought the disparities were evidence that Earth was a myth, but I now believe the opposite. In the simplest example, imagine if I asked three larrens to describe their homes. One might describe an underground complex of rooms with harsh hot winds outside and tough small shrubs clinging to life against the desert edge. Another might describe a small cottage surrounded by tall green trees next to a small waterfall. Another might describe a palace with carefully dressed stonework, fountains and gardens. Are these larrens making up stories? Of course not. They are describing the variety of circumstances that make up larren life, even on this small amount of land. If the humans inhabited the entire planet Earth as their stories claim, then the variety of circumstances would be dramatically larger.

The third reason is the strongest. If I invented a place that I wanted to convince you was real, I might have some fun and make up a few unusual details, but I would be careful not to include details that were so unusual that they undermined my credibility. My favorite example is the moon that shows up in at least 75 old stories. Piecing the stories together into a composite, we find that the moon was like a miniature planet that went around Earth, was usually seen at night, was sometimes full and bright and other times dark and barely visible, was considered to be beautiful, and made the water on Earth rise and fall. Insanity. There is nothing in our world of experience that helps us understand this. Even if they convinced us that the moon was real, why include the idea that it made the water go up and down? Unless it was true. In most of the stories, the moon is simply mentioned as a tangential detail, such as "It was an early summer evening and the full moon could occasionally be seen through the patchy clouds".

The other story I find incredible is that they claim they can jump higher here than they could on Earth. Who would even think to make up such a story?

The last core argument is that the humans exhibited behavior consistent with an overwhelming fear of extinction.

We know from some of the early stories that the humans feared that something bad had happened on Earth after they left and there was a chance they were the last humans. I, like most of my colleagues, historically viewed this as an attempt to garner our sympathy and protection. However, I reviewed thousands of pages of documents discovered at the second colony after the war and it is clear to me that the humans were focused on building redundancies. After the first Water War, there was discussion about going back to the Jadin Mountains, but they decided that their quarantine protocols did not allow for such a retreat. They debated between trying to push on to a place called Madagascar or trying to smooth things over with us. This would all be academic except that we know that in the final Water War the remaining humans staged a retreat, but that it was not in the direction they had originally come from. Rather, they disappeared out into the desert heading west by northwest. Quarantine is not a word that has survives into our current usage, but it appears to have meant splitting up a population to avoid giving each other diseases.

Think about that. The humans, when pressed in a war to the point of retreat, decided to venture out into the desert in search of another habitable land rather than risk exposing their old human companions to disease. If you feared you were among the last of your species, this might make sense. Otherwise the obvious choice would have been to return to their friends.

Also from the notes we found, we can infer that the humans split into three groups. One of those groups chose to give up all their technology, which we know from descriptions was extremely advanced. This made the other two groups very unhappy because it prevented ongoing communication (we have evidence that they could communicate with each other over great distances, although we are blind to the method). Again, this seems extreme unless their stories were true. The humans who live here now seem to be from that renegade group and we know from interrogating them that their plan was to split up every time their group hit 5000 people.

Last on this point, you will recall that the humans gave the larrens a copy of their history as a gift and "for safekeeping". This makes very little sense unless they thought there was a possibility that humans might die out and they wanted a memory of their species to remain. It was among our more shameful acts when we destroyed that copy after the Water War.

In light of these reasons, and many other less convincing reasons, I contend that the humans came to Mala about seven thousand years ago from a planet called Earth. They attempted to form a friendship with us unsuccessfully. We know there must be a habitable place beyond the desert to the east despite our failed attempts to cross it, and that the humans believed there was habitable land to the northwest.

Finally, I have to address a question that has tortured us for hundreds of years. Are the humans smarter than us? Of course, the average larren only knows the humans as they are now and would quickly answer "No!". But those of us entrusted with our old history often wonder - with both a sense of guilt for questioning larren superiority, and a sense of fear that if they are more intelligent, they will eventually rise up and be our masters. Such thoughts feed a steady drumbeat from a contingent of the college to exterminate the humans before they ever have a chance to enslave us. What can we find in the historical record?

If we accept the history as laid out earlier in the work, then it is clear that the humans mastered technology we can't fathom right now. We can't even traverse the cliffs, much less leave our planet. This would shock most larrens, but most of the technology we do have originated from the humans: watchmaking, most of our construction techniques, globe lights which we can mix but don't understand, and even writing and geometry. These were picked up from the members of the third human group that deliberately gave up technology by withholding it from the next generation as a strategy for long term survival. This suggests that their technology was so advanced that they worried it could be used to destroy them.

Of course the possession of technology does not necessarily mean they are more intelligent. Perhaps in 10,000 years larrens will have developed technology far superior to human technology. Or perhaps they took technology from other species and did not develop it themselves, or even understand it. We clearly have the benefit of longer average lives. A mature larren has twice the life experience of the average human. We have more time to consider ideas and undertake projects that last longer than a human lifetime.

In short, the historic record demonstrates that the humans possessed very advanced technology but does not answer this difficult question. However, I must end with a bitter conclusion. I believe the oral traditions are probably true which means that the humans were able to cross through space with technology that would humble us. Unless their own internal documents discovered in their colony were faked, then we have to assume that there could still be humans across the desert in possession of this same technology. I don't know why those humans have not contacted us since the Water Wars, but if they exist, then the humans are and will be a threat.

Desert
Tail
Collapsed Finger
Larren Territory
Human Territory
Speakers Rock
Myrces Village
The Knife
Lin
Echo Canyon
Desert

www.ingramcontent.com/pod-product-compliance
Lightning Source LLC
LaVergne TN
LVHW091151150826
845672LV00005B/1115

9781732017801